Spirit Seizures

Winner of

Spirit Seizures

STORIES BY
MELISSA PRITCHARD

The University of Georgia Press
ATHENS AND LONDON

© 1987 by Melissa Pritchard
Published by the University of Georgia Press
Athens, Georgia 30602
All rights reserved

Set in Galliard
The paper in this book meets the guidelines for
permanence and durability of the Committee on
Production Guidelines for Book Longevity of the
Council on Library Resources.

Printed in the United States of America

91   90   89   88   87   5   4   3   2   1

Library of Congress Cataloging in Publication Data

Pritchard, Melissa.
    Spirit seizures.

    I. Title.
PS3566.R578S6   1987   813'.54   87-5932
ISBN 0-8203-0959-1 (alk. paper)

British Library Cataloging in Publication Data available.

Some of the stories in this collection originally appeared in the *Kenyon Review*, the *Southern Review*, the *Greensboro Review*, *Prairie Schooner*, *StoryQuarterly*, the *Ontario Review*, the *Colorado Review*, *Ascent*, *Crosscurrents*, *Pulpsmith*, the *Ohio Journal*, the *Webster Review*, and *Other Voices*. The author also gratefully acknowledges the National Endowment for the Arts and the Illinois Arts Council for the assistance she received in the form of fellowships.

FOR MARK

Contents

A Private Landscape

S louched in the window seat, Deirdre dutifully reads a novel for her schoolwork. Her young face is remote, attending to more complex characters than mine.

"Tea?" I ask again.

She hesitates. "No. What are you making?"

I smack two eggs one-handedly against the bowl, a trick Mother insisted I inherit.

"Carrot cake. These carrots from last year's garden are crying to be done away with."

Deirdre's slight smile indicates that I am simple, overly concerned with food and trivialities; she goes back to her reading, her education.

I shall wind up swallowing this cake myself. Deirdre is on a health kick this week, claiming that yogurt and grapefruit juice are all she needs. Martin, in an uncharacteristically vain humor, has also gone off his feed.

Last night he commented on my weight problem. Undressing with no eye toward pleasing anybody, dropping my frayed nightgown over my head, I was unaware, until I heard his soft but disapproving words, that I was being observed from our bed, my flesh critically measured. Martin's aesthetics, I tell myself, were always sadly predictable. He wistfully watches Deirdre these days, hugs her waist tightly, strokes her long black hair while I scrape dishes and carry up laundry from the basement. Perhaps I'll move back into the guest room whenever I undress, fetch back the humble privacy I had trustingly set aside upon my marriage.

"Deirdre? Kindly remember to keep your legs together when you wear a dress."

She sighs over my prudery, and with intense exaggeration re-arranges herself in the window seat. Yesterday I requested that she not loll about the house in her bikini underwear when her father was expected home. "You're nearly fourteen years old," I said by way of justification. She shrugged and brushed wearily past me; her skin, I thought, smelled strongly of my best perfume.

* * *

After driving alongside miles of immaculate white fencing, I turn into the graveled driveway of the horse farm and pull up near the house. I walk over to the fence, rest my arms upon the top railing, watch the horses, their necks languidly dropped, mouths tearing the grass in small arcs. That bowing curve of a horse's neck suggests the prehistoric, an era comfortably free of human conflict. I wonder at such powerful animals, content to move listlessly within expensive but brittle fencing.

The owner steps out from her house and we walk across to the green and white stables. Inside, it is dim and smells strongly of hay and salt. Crossing bands of sunlight are flecked, like coarse tweed, with bits of hay and dust. Most of the stalls are vacant, but a few horses turn their heads towards us as we approach, their eyes white-rimmed, shining past us towards the open doors.

We stop in front of one stall where a dark red horse holds his head suspiciously high and tight, his ears laid back. I tentatively proffer my hand, and then withdraw it as his square lip curls back. Foul-tempered, I think, succumbing to a private notion about red horses, red anything. His eyes pitch back defiantly and I shake my head, no, not this one.

The stable phone rings, the woman excuses herself, and shielding my eyes from the cutting sunlight I walk outside again. The
pasture is sprinkled with the yellow blurs of dandelion and mild
blue wheels of chicory. Sparrows skim and cry out over the glistening backs of grazing horses. I climb a white railing and watch
as a stocky black mare trots over to another horse and gives it a sly,
aggressive nip in the rear. The bitten horse mildly moves aside and
continues grazing. Over by the highway, reduced to a fine
porcelain-like figure, stands a white horse, head lifted as though
reading the fertile spring wind. He crosses the pasture and stops
within a few yards of me. His expression is peculiarly intelligent. I
notice that his underbelly is a soft gray.

"I would like to purchase this white horse," I say as soon as the
owner finds me. We agree on a price, more than I had intended to
spend, but I know better than to bargain with fate. We discuss
terms of payment, veterinarians, places to buy tack and feed. She
promises to deliver the horse to me on the day before my daughter's fourteenth birthday.

On the drive back home I consider how Deirdre will look sitting upon the back of a pale, galloping horse, her dark hair lifting
and falling. I imagine them set against the black and green tracery
of the woods behind our property.

* * *

The box with the monogrammed blouse lies unwrapped beside
Deirdre's dinner plate. In the bathroom, all the faucets are turned
on, absorbing her disappointed sobs.

Martin is looking worried, so I finally whisper, "Go in and
comfort her, tell her next year we promise her a horse, we couldn't
afford one this year, and I'll go up to the barn and get him."

From running the slight uphill to the barn, I am breathless,
sliding back the wooden bar and stepping into the darkness. The
barn is old, with loose tongues of air between the sagging plank-
ings; it has been empty for the two years we've owned it. We are
not farmers or husbandmen, our possessions fit neatly into the

house. My garden tools stand upright in a small metal shed. Nothing overlaps.

I pick out the gleam of the white horse before the electric light abruptly halos him, his neck curved around, his eyes fixed on me. Unhitching the rope, I lead him out of the barn and down the soft, grassy path into the corral. I stroke his back, comparing its milky tint to that of the moon overhead, neither of them purely white. Against his flesh, my hand feels heavy, forgetful, and with a small, bitter feeling in me, I go back to the house.

Deirdre sits at the kitchen table, Martin holds one of his hands over hers, grateful for any contact she allows him. Eye shadow is smudged on the lids of her lowered eyes. Martin's hand is covering hers. She smiles thinly, her face blotched.

"Sorry, Mom. Still a baby about some things I guess." She looks ready to cry again, but, brave girl, crunches up another flowered Kleenex, adds it to the pile in front of her, and thanks me for the blouse.

"That's all right, darling." I bend down, kiss the top of her head.

Martin says, "Come on down to the creek with us. I'll get the flashlights and afterwards we can drive into town for some ice cream."

She winces but, still subdued from her own outburst, answers, "Sure, Dad."

The moon shines upon our property, exposing our small family. I tell Deirdre that she must shut her eyes for a minute or two. She stumbles between us and when Martin opens the corral gate I think she has guessed, but her eyes remain shut. We place her a few feet from the white horse.

"Open your eyes, darling." I am crying now. "And happy birthday!"

* * *

My original feeling for the horse had minimized; he became, for a time, an oversized pet I watched from a distance as I worked in the garden or as I backed the car down the driveway. I paid a number of expensive vet bills. My daughter persuaded me into one disastrous riding lesson under her instruction, with Martin looking on. I contrasted her vital buoyant manner with my own clumsy ability and did not ride again.

* * *

At some moment during summer's peak, the garden over-reaches its own ripeness; vegetation hangs exhausted, overcome by its own lush growth. This is my least favorite time of year, when the harvest is forgotten; unpicked tomatoes split open on trailing, imperfect vines. This is also my least favorite wedge of the afternoon, between noon and four o'clock, an empty glaring period for me. I can, with some accuracy, match my own age and season to this month and this hour. From the porch where I sit, pinned to my chair by a humidity more potent than gravity, I see the white horse, standing inert and passive. I always envisioned horses as magnificent dreamlike creatures, rearing heavenward, manes swirling like seagrass. It is not so. A horse passes its time like most anything else, placid, concerned only with whatever passes before its eyes. The horse, sapped by domesticity, confined by fences, has disillusioned me. I expected more from it.

Deirdre and Martin quarreled again last night. Instinctively, I stayed clear of their conflict, scenting its primitive, disturbing theme. The omnipotent, adored father, supplanted in the child's affections by a young stranger, in this case our neighbor's pleasant-mannered, nice-looking son.

They argued over the horse, over Deirdre's neglect of him. She goes out with her young friend, forgets to groom the horse. She rides him less and less. Martin says he is upset with her for so casually abandoning a creature who depends on her for care and affection. Of course, he has a point.

I have gone out myself to groom the horse, tugging at his mane with the metal comb, plucking out burrs from his tail, and with the curved pick prying rocks from the greenish, mossy trenches of

his hooves. I brush along the supple hills of his hips, following the
direction, the grain. I remind myself that the horse was a gift to
my daughter and that I should not long for a thing which lies
beyond my personal, private landscape.

* * *

I prattle on about a letter from an old school friend, about a
greedy crow I chased from the garden. Deirdre licks yogurt off
the tip of her spoon, then excuses herself to go and dress for her
date. Martin eats in order to be done with eating, then says he is
going out for a walk. I praise myself for not feeling hurt that I am
uninvited and dump dishes in the sink, wipe down counters, and
feel vexed that no one thought to help me. But I never ask for
help, or even demand it; I wish to appear self-sufficient before my
family, because I suspect I am not. Damn. I turn off the water,
leave the kitchen undone, and go after my husband in the summer
twilight.

In the middle of the creek we sit on rocks as bleached and flattened as the horse's flank I brushed this morning. Martin snaps a
dry stick into pieces, letting each bit drop into the swirling water
and take its course. He flicks the last chip of wood; it lodges between our two stones, resisting the current of water.

Martin looks tired. The loss of weight from his recent diet has
not improved him; it has left him slack, gaunt.

Plunging my arm into the softly buckling water, I am shocked
by its coldness.

"I asked Deirdre to stop going about the house in her underwear when you're home."

I am remembering Martin's criticisms as I undressed in our
bedroom that night, and hold my wet, reddened hand up to the
sky.

"Sometimes I almost hate her."

I climb awkwardly over to my husband and crouch down. He
puts an arm around me, draws me close. Needing comfort, we sit

upon a large flat stone, until we become cramped and stiff from sitting so motionless, surrounded by water.

Walking home in the dark, without a flashlight, I trip across a fallen cottonwood tree, bruising my shin on its upreaching tangled root. Martin is concerned and helps me up.

Back home, relieved that our house is emptied of her, we make oddly exuberant love. Afterward we are reserved toward one another, sitting up late, drinking brandies, and reading fiction, the light steady between our two chairs, waiting for Deirdre.

* * *

One-thirty and she has not come home. Martin, furious with me for not knowing the address of the party she has gone to, is in the kitchen, watching television and thinking about calling the police. In the living room I am trying to understand the jealousy and resentment I feel towards my only child. When the telephone rings, Martin answers, comes into the doorway.

"She wants you. She wants to talk to you."

In a crisis she has always reached for me.

I wave a signal to Martin that she is all right.

"Deirdre, please, stop it. Stop crying now. It's all right."

Martin sets down a pencil, a pad of paper, and I write down the address she gives me.

"Ok, honey, hang on, we'll be there in about twenty minutes. Yes, Daddy's fine. He's right here and he's just fine."

Martin is gone. Looking through the house, I discover him in Deirdre's room, a place he has seldom entered, respectful of his child's privacy. Now he is bent over her dressing table, holding open a grocery sack, and all of it, cosmetics, mirrors, ribbons, hair rollers, all the paraphernalia of a young female, is tumbling into the bag. When the dressing table is bare, he goes to the bulletin board above her bed and tears down pictures of rock stars and movie stars. They float, without a change of expression, into the grocery bag. Martin takes the bag outside, sets it inside the garbage can, and we drive into town to find Deirdre. She sits in the back seat on the way home, and none of us says anything.

Sitting on the edge of her bed, I apologize and try to explain for Martin, and I am the one who smooths her dark hair. She has lately denied me this power to comfort her and hungrily I draw her back into myself. She relates a small, scattered story of betrayal and jealousy at a teenage party. I am proud that she defended the values we taught her, but with apprehension I read her expression, which tells me that one day she will risk a different choice, hurting us in the process. But now she says she loves me and, believing her, I leave Deirdre sleeping and safe again, a recovered part of my own self.

In the dark living room Martin, at a loss in his own house, is staring out of a window.

"She's fine," I say lightly. "You'd be proud of her." I feel myself the center of the family once again, though this is temporary power, splinted and artificial. He answers only that he is exhausted and is going to bed.

The late summer moon, like a veined marble bowl, spills out an abundance of light. I walk up the hill to the barn, take down the saddle, the bridle, and go back down to the corral. "Here," I say, "come here, hey," and the white horse, splashed with shadow, moves over to me. Calmly, I slip the bit and the bridle over him and cinch up the saddle. I have watched Deirdre do this many times. He absorbs my clumsiness as I climb up on his broad back.

Passing out of the corral gate, I see the house where my daughter and my husband sleep in rooms broken off from each other. I turn away from them and ride unburdened through damp grasses, straying from those boundaries set by daylight, by marriage, by family, by the erosion of time upon my private life.

With an urge to swiftness, the horse gallops forward and forward into the humid and calling darkness. A wildness begins to rise up in me when I glimpse the uprooted cottonwood, the tree I had fallen across earlier this evening.

In steady, lulling rhythm the white horse goes straight for it, his breath drawing in and out of the moist swell of his lungs. We rise dreamlike, above the tree, both of us soaring up, freed from the heavy, clinging earth.

Not far away, glittering like falseness, runs the silver and black cord of creek water, which, even in this particular season, is considered pure, quite excellent for our family to drink.

Companions

S ure a shame," the Christian boy said, his hand timidly patting her bad hip. He thrust out his own legs and looked down at them. They were whole and of even lengths.

He wrapped his arm politely around her. "Jesus healed the lame ones. I'll bet he could heal you, too."

Suddenly he sat straight up and grasped both her hands. "Lora Lee, Lora Lee, do you believe Jesus can heal you?"

"No," Lolly answered plainly. "No, I don't."

The miracles of Jesus were wondrously inspiring, and he was puzzled by Lolly's lame hip and faithless attitude. In his experience, persons with ailments turned readily to the Lord. It was the well ones, while they still had some wholeness left, who kept away.

One morning he stopped to see Lolly again and found her asleep. He removed the outer layer of his clothing and decided he'd better leave on his underwear for protection. Climbing on top of her he rocked himself up and down in an odd, miserable way. Moments later, when he backed out of the door, his clothing held in front of his wretched face, Lolly chose to lie. She spoke softly, saying yes, she had faith that Jesus could heal anybody's lameness. Then she yelled out that He could probably forgive anybody just about anything at all.

Convinced that the Christian, in such a disappointing way, had got her pregnant, Lolly Fairchild quit her typing class and spitefully wrote home the news, including the small detail that she would be home on the 11:45 P.M. bus, and could her mother please be there to meet her.

She plugged her Turkish taffy into the ashtray, slid the cover over it until it jammed, stood up, and limped to the back of the bus. Although the cubicle smelled of disinfectant, Lolly was cautious, as her mother had taught, not to lower her weight onto the toilet seat. Germs and filth, said Mrs. Fairchild, were the devil's legion. Lolly stood up and spit out the sweet taffy taste.

Most people Lolly passed as she went back up the aisle were trying to sleep, their coats laid over their laps. A figure seated beside a window switched on the tiny overhead light.

"Pull up a seat, dear." The man's face was as pocked and dry as pumice; his navy-blue watch cap was yanked down nearly to his eyebrows. Lolly stayed where she was.

"Harvey," he said, "Harvey Spidwell's my name. Why ain't you asleep like everybody else? Well, since you're harmless enough, maybe I'll show you something." He began unbuttoning his brown and red plaid jacket. "There we go. There's my boy. This here is . . ." He lifted out the little dog. "Mr. Matador. He is full-bred chihuahua. Sits inside my coat pocket. Sleeps there. Go on, you pet him. He's friendly. About a year ago I got him in trade for an old pair of boots and a set of Christmas lights. Go on now and pet him."

Harvey stroked the dog with his hand, a hand which Lolly thought more remarkable than the dog. The thumb was gone down to the knuckle, and the skin across the top of his hand looked like it had stewed and boiled for quite a while. Lolly did not reach out to touch the dog.

"Does it do tricks?" she asked feebly.

"Tricks? Nope. The only trick Mr. Matador does is to scratch on my chest when he has to relieve himself. And I got to be quick to find him a place to go." Harvey grinned.

"Oh," said Lolly. "Why do you keep him if he's such a trouble?"

The dog was sitting dejectedly in Harvey's lap.

"Dearheart, he is not one speck of pain. He's less bother than I am to myself. Let me tell you something. A man has got to have a companion. A man has got to have one living thing that he thinks of beyond his own damned self. Otherwise, he's no darn better off than dead. For instance, I'll bet you have a boyfriend somewhere that you dress up for, try to please."

Lolly shook her head.

"Well then, you got to have something that makes you care enough to wake up, get yourself dressed, and repeat your business every day. Everybody does. What is it then, religion or a baby?"

Lolly sat down beside him. "A baby."

"There. I could have told you. I'm a good guesser. Now how old is it, this baby of yours, and boy or girl?"

She looked down and covered her perfectly flat belly with her chapped hand. "It hasn't been born to me yet." And I'll bet, she thought, it's about the size of a ten-cent jawbreaker.

Mr. Matador, dancing on his hind legs, pawed frenziedly at the window.

"You're young yet to have a little one, ain't you? Sixteen, seventeen, what?"

"Well, I'm going home and my mother will be helping me, I'm sure."

The man shrugged and reached under the seat to grab a paper sack with a green bottle neck sticking out of it. He offered it to her and Lolly made a face. "Suit yourself. We all do in this world." He unscrewed the black cap, tipped his head back, and drank.

His profile was upturned to the dim light, and Lolly could see that part of his face, like his hand, was scarred and red, horrible looking. By noon Harvey Spidwell must be a monster. He kept on swallowing, gulping, seeming not to notice her stare. Laboriously, he twisted the cap back on and stuffed the bag under his seat. He turned to her with a sly expression.

"Well now, could I answer my thirst that quick if I had a kid with me or a woman for that matter? Let me tell you something. A dog is loyal. A dog don't talk back at you, and it don't try to run every minute of your life. A dog is grateful for whatever you do for it, deeply grateful. The less a dog gets, the sooner it licks your hand for what do come along. People, on the other hand, the more they get, the less satisfied they are. Man is a spoiled animal, a jealous animal. You hear me well. Man is a beast and dog is a beast, but a man is not a dog."

With that he turned from her and looked out into the fields unrolling like dark patterned linoleum. Lolly heard him muttering to himself. He seemed to have forgotten her.

Lolly stood up and said good-bye. Harvey didn't appear to hear her. He went on cursing out the window while he held the little dog, his ruined hand stroking its small, smooth back.

The trouble with him, she decided, switching on the light above her seat and flopping open her magazine, was that dumb dog was the only thing he cared about. Just listen to him, cussing all the world as it goes by. He must be crazy. Then she imagined some kind of an accident, fire on her face, making her skin melt like grease running down a plate. It was terrible. Much worse than her bad hip. People pitied her but they weren't repulsed. She was sure that he disgusted people. At least, she thought proudly, she would have herself a baby to care for.

The bus turned into the station a few minutes after midnight. Lolly held her suitcase, waiting for the door to open. The driver made a long sucking noise with his mouth that made her stumble as she descended the steps. No one else had gotten off the bus.

The tiny station seemed deserted. There was one man in an orange T-shirt and a baseball cap asleep in a chair by the door. Lolly walked into the cafeteria. A small woman sat alone at one of

the tables, calmly dipping into a goblet of pudding. Her mother
lifted the spoon to her mouth daintily, as if all the world were
watching her, until she must have sensed Lolly watching her, for
she turned around and lowered her spoon, all at the same time.
Her daughter limped across the room, between the tables, and
Mrs. Fairchild made no move to greet her. Her face was quiet as
paper, as cool and cold as if it had been slipped from a dark drawer
into the light. Hazel Fairchild waited until the girl stood exactly
in front of her and then reached up, her white glove sliding softly
across Lolly's cheek. "Shame," she said. Without a word, she
finished her tapioca, scraping the sides of the goblet.

Even another human being growing inside of her did not make
Lolly feel distinct from her mother anymore. Her mother was
stronger than ever.

As Mrs. Fairchild unlocked her car door in the parking lot, she
said a second thing to her daughter. "Your hair looks a sight."

When the ride was over, Lolly took her suitcase and followed
her mother back into their house.

"Are you or are you not carrying a man's seed?"

Lolly chose not to answer her mother. She was busy tying her
knee socks into matched knots and lining them up in the top
drawer of her dresser.

Mrs. Fairchild began to fan her face with the letter.

"Who is this man?"

"Why, he's a perfectly good Christian."

"A fine, smart answer, Lora Lee. And who isn't a Christian in
this part of the world?"

"Myself, maybe," Lolly mumbled.

"What's that? Speak properly. You sound as if you're buried
headfirst in a flour sack."

Lolly dreamily traced a design on the perfumed drawer paper.

"I said I am not accompanying you to church tomorrow."

Her mother hooted, unbelieving.

"And I'm not going out to Daddy's grave again, neither."

In Mrs. Fairchild's judgment, if a certain person wasn't worth respecting when he was alive and underfoot, at least he was owed some respect now that he was dead and out of the way. Lora Lee was clearly in a state of rebellion, and although she had never hesitated to raise a hand to her daughter, why, at the moment Lora Lee was spiteful enough to strike her mother back. So Mrs. Fairchild said, "I'm going to call Dr. Sturgis."

Lolly slammed the drawer shut on her socks. "That doctor is an idiot and I won't be having one particle of my body subjected to him. His hands sweat, besides."

"Since when did you become so particular about somebody's hands on one particle or the other of you, sweet girl?"

Lolly's face puckered, and her mother, feeling uncertain, watched her sniffle and knot and unknot a pair of red plaid knee socks she had neglected to put away. My family has brought me to ruin, she thought. First my husband, by wallowing like a hog in sin and to my complete embarrassment dying because of it, and now his offspring telling me she's pregnant by some perfectly good Christian she can't even name. I scarcely believe her.

She viewed her daughter with a kind of pitying censure, unable to imagine what sort of fool would take the trouble to pursue Lolly, with her milktoast features and crippled leg. Why couldn't her one child, her only child, have taken after her a bit?

She stepped into the bedroom and delicately dropped her daughter's letter into the wastebasket. Before going out to call the doctor, she stopped and rearranged, according to color, the stuffed dogs on Lolly's bed.

Lolly accompanied her mother on the drive out to Mr. Fairchild's grave.

"Dr. Sturgis says you are not pregnant. He says, in fact, that you are still a virgin. I don't know why, but he seemed surprised. He also says you have a tiny cyst, about the size of a nickel, in there. I don't understand, Lora Lee, why you deliberately set out to cause me such an upset. When the doctor spoke to me I was so thankful. Land sakes, we'd have had to pack up what few things we . . ."

"Oh, be quiet. What does he know?" Lolly's face was turned to the window.

Lolly's mother stretched out her hand to discipline her daughter, but thought better of it and replaced her gloved hand on the wheel.

Lolly was disappointed. Now she had no proof that anyone found her attractive. Besides, a baby would have been all hers. She would have had something tiny and helpless to care for. Dejected, Lolly slumped over in her seat.

"Sit up, child. A baby is a terrible burden. Most people are simply ill-prepared for a child. Not to mention that most people who have babies make a decent attempt to see a minister beforehand."

From what she had been told by her aunt the summer she turned twelve, Lolly knew for a fact that her own mother had been both ill-prepared and burdened by her birth.

Mr. Fairchild, Lolly had heard from her mother's sister, who sat at their kitchen table one afternoon while she baby-sat Lolly, pouring them both cups of tea and dumping sugar into each cup while she talked, had died of cancer of the testicles. She rolled her eyes and measured the size of a grapefruit with her hands. "One of 'em swole up this big, and that dark little back porch where he was, smelled to high heaven, and your mother, tending to him day after day, from one month to the next, and pregnant to boot. Yes, you din't know that? Well, it's like her not to tell. Till, angel that she was, she smelled nearly as bad as that . . ." Here she measured the grapefruit size again. "And her eyes were circled with his sickness and you, imagine it if you please, a tadpole, wrinkled and swelling up inside her, taking what little strength she had left to herself. Just think of it, two things to care for and while one of 'em's growing, the other's dying, one to be born, one buried. Praise God . . ." She trailed off, then reached over with the teapot and with her great purple arm slopped out another cup for herself. She rolled on in confidential, breathless tones. "If I was her, which thankfully I was not, I would have sent that man aways somewhere to do his rotting and dying. He weren't no good to her alive or dying and he's not much good to her now that he's fully dead, neither. The Lord served him a justice with such a high, stinking disease. It's a pity you never knowed him, Lora Lee, or you'd have witnessed that I speak the truth." She slapped the table with her huge, maculated paw. "Praise the justice of the Lord."

Lolly stared at her solemnly, pulled her finger from her mouth, rolled it in the sugar bowl, put her finger back into her mouth, and sucked hard.

They turned into the small cemetery. Twice a month, usually after church, they came here to "tidy up the plot," as her mother put it. For Lolly, the people who rested here, close beside her own flesh and blood, were her father's neighbors, present but remote.

Mrs. Fairchild parked under the diseased elm tree, switched off the motor, yanked up the brake, and looked at Lolly. "You and I should thank God in church tomorrow. You have learnt your lesson without having to pay a high price. With honor intact, we will carry on as before. With one exception."

Pulling off her white gloves, Mrs. Fairchild drew on the canvas garden gloves, imprinted with round red radishes and tiny orange carrots. "I have spoken with that Mrs. Stoof, the beauty operator, and she has kindly made available a position for you at the Golden Pavilion. She's offered to hire you on, which in my estimation is sheer good fortune to which we must be thankful, since most of her girls come from the city with certificates from beauty college. She needs someone immediately and has expressed her willingness to take you on. You're to be there, punctually, on Monday morning. You will be responsible for keeping your own uniform clean."

Lolly had taken a map from the glove compartment and was reading it with studied interest.

"I am sure that once you are settled in there, you will be grateful."

Mrs. Fairchild, neatly puncturing the grass with her spiked heels, walked over to the little liver-colored headstone. She carried garden clippers and King Alfred daffodils wrapped in green florist's paper. Lolly sat in the car, the map stretched across her lap like a napkin, while her mother bent down, clipping tufts of grass from around the marble tablet. She jammed the daffodils into the sunken vase behind the headstone and without a glance at the other graves stripped off her gloves and walked back to the car.

Lolly had never seen anyone else approach a grave with garden gloves, grass clippers, and, on occasion, a can of weed killer, but her mother was uniquely disturbed by disorder. The natural world's tendency to reproduce and decay insured a continual clutter which kept Mrs. Fairchild compulsively busy. She attacked any suggestion of fertility or sprawling decline with an arsenal of home remedies and utensils. Whatever lay within her reach was rigorously pruned according to her own drastic sense of proportion. She snipped the labels out of her clothes, replacing them with labels from expensive shops. She read advice to Lolly from outdated etiquette books as if they were scriptural lessons, and marched her daughter to church in white gloves and pastel flats, taking pains to hand-hem her dresses to a length, however unfashionable, that she maintained would soften Lolly's limp. She prided herself, and said so, on not galloping after the latest fads, holding instead to what she called the eternal pillars of good taste and decency. And she was determined to raise herself above the common riffraff of society from which, unfortunately, she was descended.

"Character deficiency or bodily weakness, no good ever came of anyone's showing off their helplessness to the world. Defects such as yours are best kept private, best hidden or dressed up to look unlike themselves," Hazel Fairchild would pronounce, rubbing a perfect bull's-eye of rouge onto each of Lolly's cheeks, then yanking the sash around her waist until Lolly gasped. "Always present your best face and figure to this world. Life is unkind to misfits."

"Hold them straight out."

Lolly extended her hands, and in the critical ensuing silence put them back in her lap. She had one shovel-shaped fingernail left; the rest had been bitten off the night before, as she lay in bed, trying to realize that what she had inside her was not a baby at all but a growth about the size of a nickel.

"So it's Hazel's daughter." Mrs. Stoof squinted at Lolly. It was eight o'clock Monday morning, an hour and a half before the first customer would arrive for a shampoo and set.

"Look like that . . ." She jerked her head toward the mirror where Lolly was not well reflected. "And you couldn't pay a customer to sit still for you."

Lolly didn't need to be told of her disappointing effect on people. Her mother reminded her of it every time she jabbed a lock of hair behind Lolly's ear, buttoned the top button of her sweater, or with a cluck of dissatisfaction brushed lint off her dark blue skirt.

"You're a fine girl, but your mother, forgive me for saying so and I'll get to the point, lives in her own oddball world. There's no reason for you to stay there with her, just so's to keep her company. Charlene, shag over here and help this young lady out. This is Hazel Fairchild's daughter."

Charlene glided over in her dirty, spotted pink uniform. Her black, puffed-up hair had a frizzled yellow streak straight down the middle, causing Lolly to think of a skunk dropping dead off a tree limb and landing itself right side up on this woman's head. Charlene's bright blue eyes were rimmed in black, like Cleopatra decals. Lolly wondered if Charlene had ever heard of Egypt.

Mrs. Stoof studied Charlene and in particular fixed her eye on a small pink roller dangling from the back of her head.

"That chunky little woman Mrs. Anderson tells me she wants her hair styled approximate to yours, which proves there's no accounting for poor taste in this town."

Charlene snapped her chewing gum and grinned, her skinny hands testing and holding out strands of Lolly's lank hair. Mrs. Stoof went off to unlock the register, while Charlene set to work, muttering about never having enough time to get herself fixed up right.

Reluctantly, Lolly entered the small-town backwash of current fashion. Her head was jerked backwards, scrubbed and rinsed over a pink washbasin by a grumbling Charlene. Her scalp was intersected with skinny aluminum clips. Wet pieces of hair dropped like question marks to the floor, and the rest was stuck around pink rubber rollers. Her cuticles were folded back with an orange stick, her sore nails brushed with Hot Mango Frost. For forty-five minutes she dozed under the roaring plastic dome of a hairdryer, gripping an old issue of *National Geographic*. By 9:15, seated in front of the mirror, she was unrecognizable. Charlene popped her gum faster, giving the final touches to Lolly's hairstyle with a rattail comb, while Lolly's narrow face, like a pale insubstantial wafer, receded under its artifice.

Physical transformations inspire beauticians, and Mrs. Stoof and Charlene were deeply moved as they stood over Lolly's image in the mirror.

"A diamond in the raw," Mrs. Stoof said.

"Rough," Charlene corrected, leaning as close to the mirror as her nose would allow, scratching violet shadow along the crease of her eyelid.

"What do you say, Lolly?" Mrs. Stoof asked.

"My mother will have a stroke" was all Lolly said.

Lolly limped about beside Mrs. Stoof and Charlene for the rest of the day, convinced that she would never be able to flatter all these women, not one of whom seemed pleased with herself. While Mrs. Stoof never lost her ability to please, the effort to revive and reconstruct her customers clearly told on Charlene, who, though careless and short on tact, was surprisingly popular. By the end of the day, with her hair unkempt, her makeup smeared, and her disposition surly, she still winked at Lolly in the mirror while her customer's eyes were shut, as though it were all a joke, winding up curls on such irritable tinted heads.

In the Golden Pavilion, where nothing was golden except the flecks in the formica countertops, Lolly's limp attracted little attention. Mrs. Teasdale and Mrs. Castle spoke with one another in the mirror, they fussed over their hair and compared their faces; no one was concerned with an irreparable defect of the leg. Amid violent pink fixtures, roaring hairdryers and spray cans shooting forth vaporous mists, conversation languished. No one had a comment for Lolly's bad hip, and for that she was grateful and therefore pleased by her new position.

Sometime after Lolly had been employed as an uncertified beautician at the Golden Pavilion, and heard plenty from Charlene about what a nice looking but luckless man Mr. Fairchild had been, and how the whole town had known about his interest in the pharmacist's cashier, who had long since married and moved out of town, Lolly's mother, due to no particular cause or grievance, had a stroke.

At first Lolly cherished the bit of freedom brought on by her mother's paralysis. Mrs. Fairchild could not say one word to stop Lolly from doing whatever it pleased her to do. Lolly let her uniform go unwashed, she tinted the color and rearranged the style of her hair several times. She wore jewelry and bought scarves. But caring for an invalid soon imposed a routine on Lolly's life and she began to feel more controlled by her mother than ever.

Having a limp never got in the way of anybody else, but a body that could do nothing for itself but sleep and digest tyrannized other people completely. And now it was her mother's birthday, an occasion which Hazel always had made a particular fuss over, since "No one else," she would sniff injuredly, daubing at her temples with a cologned handkerchief, "would ever, ever bother." So Lolly felt obliged to stir up some sort of a celebration.

Lolly pinched her mother's nostrils shut with her left hand while she whizzed the can of hairspray around her head. Hazel sat like an offended angel, eyes squeezed shut, wreaths of perfumed vapor around her head.

Lolly dropped the can down on the littered table. "There you go, cute as a postcard." She released her mother's nose; Mrs. Fairchild opened her eyes and blinked. Finding a hand mirror with a blue plastic rim, Lolly held its oily wavy surface a few inches from her mother's face.

"Like it?"

Her mother wagged her finger twice, a signal which indicated no. Her hair looked as if tiny rust-colored bedsprings had been set loose all over her skull. At regular intervals, like an artificially planted forest, patches of white scalp shone through.

"And now . . ." Lolly drew an envelope from the pocket of her soiled pink uniform. "Here's a birthday greeting signed by all the girls except Coral, who's a Jehovah's Witness. She says they don't believe in birthdays."

She showed her mother the signatures scattered inside the card.

"Here's Charlene's. It says, 'I'm gonna wash that man right outta your hair . . .' Some joke between you two, I gather. Charlene adds that she misses your Thursday appointments."

Her mother nodded, the good half of her face reflecting her pleasure that someone thought kindly of her, the paralyzed half long and bleak as a sidewalk.

"Now, Mamma, don't run off. Charlene and I came up with the grandest idea for a birthday present you've ever seen. Shut your eyes now."

Her mother obediently closed her eyes.

"Keep 'em shut and don't peek or I'll have to fetch a dish towel to wrap around your head and it'll spoil your hairdo!" Lolly disappeared from the room while her mother sat in her blue bed jacket, waiting.

Lolly returned, carrying a large box with air holes punched in the top and a big red satin bow flopping off the sides. She set the box on her mother's lap.

"Ok. Happy birthday. Open your eyes."

Hazel Fairchild's eyes remained shut.

"Open your eyes now, Ma!"

Her mother started. She had drifted asleep, waiting for her surprise.

Mrs. Fairchild's hands trembled helplessly among the ribbons until Lolly couldn't watch anymore and reached over and jerked the bow off the box herself. The box rocked a little in Mrs. Fairchild's lap. The lid began to slide off and a dog's head popped up out of the darkness, its eyes bulging in fright.

Mrs. Fairchild's face looked ready to split down the middle. Her hand reached out to touch the animal.

Lolly played with the red ribbon, wrapping it around and around her wrist like a tourniquet. The dog's front paws were on the edge of the box and it sprang out of its nest of tissue paper.

"It's a baby chihuahua, Ma."

The puppy tripped listlessly around the rumpled bed, as though looking for a spot to relieve itself. Lolly noticed her mother's expression and hurriedly plunked the dog back into its box.

"I'll take him out for a minute. He's probably nervous."

Her mother bobbled her head gratefully.

"Now comes your biggest surprise!"

Lolly came back in with her mother's old turquoise coat and a mixed bunch of plastic flowers.

"Just guess what! We are going to visit Daddy!" She saw by her mother's alarmed expression that Hazel was afraid to leave her room.

"Oh yes we are," said Lolly, as firmly as a nurse. She lifted the color television off its stand and pushed the shining golden cart with the black wheels over to the bed.

"It's my second birthday present. You haven't gone out to see Daddy since your sickness, and this time I'll trim the grass and put up the flowers. And don't fret about how I'm going to get you out there."

She tugged the coat over her mother's body and then lifted her off the bed and slid her onto the TV cart. Mrs. Fairchild whimpered as she was wheeled out to the car, the plastic flowers bouncing in her lap.

"Now where's Baby-Dog got to?" The chihuahua ran out from underneath the car and licked Lolly's bare ankle. She set him on the car seat between herself and her mother, where he sat panting and alert.

While she was driving, Lolly saw her mother furtively shove the flowers onto the floor. Lolly sighed.

"The rules have got to change now, Ma. Fresh flowers don't keep worth a darn even with an aspirin in the water. These plastic ones, they'll be fresh even on Christmas Day, fresh as the day I picked 'em. I never understood why you didn't take to 'em, being as opposed to decay as you are. Dying flowers are not a happy sight, especially not to the dead. Look, I brought your clippers and old garden gloves. You can sit by and watch while I make Daddy comfortable. I expect he's been lonely with no one out to visit him, don't you? I found a picture of Daddy in the attic the other day. He was nearly handsome, don't you think?"

Lolly was driving carefully, but she felt a rising urge to talk, to reveal to her mother what she knew.

"Charlene talks a lot, you know, and she says Daddy was a real ladies man. She says he really knew how to pluck compliments straight from the air, even for old Mrs. Purcell at the post office, and sound as if he meant every sugar-bit of it. At least he was good for something, was what I thought when I heard it. I guess that young lady that was a cashier at the pharmacy used to come by quite a lot of Daddy's praise before she had to move away and before he got ill and you had to take care of him, while being so pregnant with me and all."

She snuck a look at her mother and pulled off the road.

"I'm sorry, Ma. Calm down. I said I'm sorry. I just wish I'd known Daddy for myself. I've got to think there was something good about him, even if that something hurt you. Now, you want me to take you along out to the cemetery? I'll trim the grass real nice while you sit and watch. And you'll see . . ." Lolly reached down and retrieved the bouquet. "These flowers will look pretty, they honestly will look real from a distance, from where you'll be sitting, you'll swear they're as real as anything. Don't cry, Ma."

Mrs. Fairchild watched from the car while Lolly took the flowers and the clippers and the gloves and walked the short distance to Mr. Fairchild's burying place. The chihuahua sniffed frantically among the headstones, while Lolly knelt and clipped the long grass. The grass was more overgrown than she had ever seen it, and it took some work to clear it away. She also had to keep pushing the dog's wet nose out of the way.

"Little pest," she muttered.

She decided there was little difference in clipping the grass around a tombstone and clipping the hair around someone's neck. It also occurred to her that her mother's hair had stopped growing since her stroke. Lolly worked nervously. She felt as though she were kneeling on her father's chest. She crawled around and jabbed the flowers in the vase behind the headstone and decided they looked pretty but not at all realistic.

Stripping off the gloves, she stood up and walked back to the car. "Baby-Dog!" she called.

The puppy was trotting around Mr. Fairchild's neatly trimmed grave, sniffing as though its lungs would burst. Lolly called again. Baby-Dog trotted behind the marble slab to the vase and cocked his leg up on the plastic flowers.

"He's so dumb to do that," Lolly said. She did not dare look over at her mother.

The drive home was silent except for the dog heaving up some bits of grass and mucus onto the car seat, which smelled terrible.

As she lifted and pushed her mother back onto the TV cart, Lolly saw that Mrs. Fairchild seemed extremely weak and dejected. In her room she lay across the bed, eyes fluttering, breathing unsteadily. When Lolly asked if she might like some tomato with rice soup or a cup of tea, Mrs. Fairchild didn't even have the energy to wag her finger in the signal which meant thank you, no. So Lolly gently switched off the light and left her mother in darkness.

Mrs. Fairchild could not have invented a more fitting reprimand for her daughter's tasteless birthday celebration. The dog had upset her and her husband's past revolted her. When Lolly walked into Hazel's room shortly after eleven o'clock, she found her mother in the aftermath of a second stroke.

Lora Lee adopted a calm, first-aid attitude. She drew the blankets right up under Mrs. Fairchild's shocked chin and tuned the radio to a station with pleasant soothing music. When the dog lunged up onto the bed, she dutifully tossed him out into the hall. She sat on the edge of the bed and, taking the hair brush from the night table, fluffed up her mother's hair a bit. With professional gravity, she examined her mother's hands and pushed at the cuticles. She thought of herself alone in the world, with the defective walk she had inherited from her parents' unhappy union, and felt like crying for herself. She wanted her mother to tell her what to do next, but her mother seemed quite speechless and beyond giving Lolly any more bits of advice. In fact, she seemed about to desert Lolly. But then Lolly would do what children have always and rightfully done. She would choose to leave her mother before her mother could take leave of her.

She telephoned and woke the doctor. She also called her aunt, who huffed, complained of her heart, then said she would be delighted to drive twenty-five miles to sit beside her younger sister. Lolly started to dial for an ambulance, then set down the phone and went into her room.

Besides her few clothes and the photograph, there was little else to put into her suitcase. In the hall closet she found a plaid hatbox, took it into the kitchen, and punched six air holes for Baby-Dog. She took out her mother's green felt hat and the mothcake.

Finally, Lolly dialed the ambulance service. While she waited for someone to answer, she heard music playing on the other end of the line. The same music was coming from the radio in her mother's room. She hung up the phone.

Finding the dog under the kitchen table licking the floor, she sat him in the hatbox and zipped it shut. The dog yelped and dug his nails through the tissue paper. "Hush," Lolly said.

Opening the front door and picking up the hatbox and her suitcase, she stepped outside into the darkness. As she walked in the direction of the bus station, she heard in the silence between her uneven footsteps high-pitched, faraway children's voices. RAIN, RAIN, STEP ON A CRACK . . . RIDE A COCKHORSE . . . BAA BAA BLACK SHEEP, HAVE YOU ANY WOOL?

She nodded to the bus driver. With the dog asleep beside her and the bus moving away fast, Lolly switched on the light, un-latched her small half-empty suitcase, and took out the photograph of Mr. Fairchild, who had not once, since the day Lolly discovered him like this, stopped smiling at her.

She poked torn bits of the photograph deep down in the ashtray. Now her mother and her father could be the way they had been, however they had been, before their daughter was born.

And this time she, Lolly, would choose her own companions. Carefully.

A Dying Man

My wife is no liberated bitch. Like me, she was raised in the old way, to be true to her nature. If I ask Merle, my mistress, why she cannot prepare a delicate gravy like Hedy's, she says, "There's no gravy in my character; I am not a gravy character."

Today I am sick, quite ill and out of sorts. Hedy speaks to the doctor on the telephone, her voice hard and crisp as a cabbage rim. I worry her. When you are old, a sneeze can open the door on death itself. I have a pension; Hedy could take it and go live with her sister. But she and her sister argue. No, Hedy should stay alone here and go to her church meetings and struggle with her little budget and sigh dejectedly in her sleep. If she complained out loud, she knows that, even dead, I would hear her.

She comes into the room, bringing my supper tray.

"What are you doing? Sleeping?"

"Yes, a bit."

"The doctor stops tomorrow on his way to the office."

"Ach."

"What? I am at my wit's end trying to care for you, not knowing what is the matter. You watch TV, for one thing. You never watched the TV before. If you had gout or the mumps I would know what to do."

"I told you what is wrong. I am old and I am dying."

"Oh ho. Listen to him. Your grandfather lived until what, eighty-seven years old, your grandmother ninety something. She died at the sink, dropped her toothbrush. It was practically the first thing you told me about yourself."

"All my uncles had weak hearts."

She is propping pillows behind my back, smoothing the sheets. Then she sets the tray across my lap. For dessert there are three Viennese crescents on a white plate with blue flowers. Morning glory flowers. I eat the cookies first.

"I have a church meeting tonight. I'm thinking I should not leave you here alone." She is stacking magazines on the night-stand. Slap, slap. She is a noisy thing. "I should stay here with you and play cards. Rummy." Boom. She slams a drawer shut.

"Don't stay for me. Please, you go out. On the way home, maybe stop in the drugstore for some breath mints and a TV guide."

"All right." She stands and pats her hair in the vanity mirror. "I'll go then."

She takes the tray.

* * *

On first acquaintance with Hedy, I got her piggledy-drunk until she vomited on the tablecloth at the café and howled like a cat the whole way home. Now, as she says, she doesn't touch the stuff; still, she slops rum into the leckerlein and into that hideous fruit-cake of hers. But these are ordinary memories.

My wife comes in, tugging on her gloves, wearing her leather coat with the raccoon collar. She kisses me on the forehead, pre-sumptuously maternal for a woman with no children.

When I was a boy, I would crouch on the kitchen floor, beating the kettle bottom with wooden ladles. Boom boom boom boom, marching to war, while mother moved from the counter to the stove, chopping and stirring, her dark hair sticking to her damp cheeks. I would perch in her lap while she read aloud, and I could never separate my delight in her stories from my pleasure in being buried in her material, her scent.

Odd. Last night I remembered the bed I used to sleep in as a child in my mother's house, felt the weight of the blankets; even the smell of starched sheets was evident to me. I traced the wall's design, blue drums, red horses, dark eyeless soldiers, then wept, jealously recalling the drab but precious view from my window, the hopeful way I got dressed each morning.

As a result of the weeping, I suppose, I began to feel mother's caresses, as unavoidably as I had remembered my childhood's bed. I started to dread what was before me in this bed, if not now, then later. Blurred women bending over me, talking softly to one another, appearing, disappearing, no longer pretending to obey me.

✶ ✶ ✶

I open my eyes to see who it is, reaching through the opening of my pajamas.

"He is so sweet," she whispers.

"Leave me alone. Sit up. How did you get in?"

"Aren't you happy to see me? Delighted? We have an hour together."

"How did you get in here?"

"The key."

"Hedy nearly didn't go out tonight. You might have walked in while she was here. We would have been playing cards. Rummy."

"Well, that would have been awkward, wouldn't it? Aren't you pleased that I'm here?"

Merle stands up and removes her Persian lamb jacket. She is wearing a peacock blue dress with a wide leopard belt. Her uneven makeup, shiny as crayola, is not so unsuited to a person starved on his wife's severity.

"Pretty dolled up tonight."

She moves around the room as though she has picked up my

own anxious mood and finally stops at a window with a view of a red brick apartment building. She lays her gloves on the windowsill. Under the bedclothes, I cup my hands over my genitals.

"I thought about bringing you flowers or a paperback."

"I don't need gifts, thank you." Stiff sounding but there it is. Hedy's order, Hedy's morality, Hedy's nature inhabits this room.

Merle sits beside me on the bed. I want to squeeze her powdered face.

"What's wrong? A cold?"

"Nothing. A weakness."

"You're pale as goosemeat."

"Goosemeat?" I smile. "But you, you look wonderful. A regular dolly."

The fact is, I can't recall how to behave with her and am feeling panicky.

"Want to kiss me?"

"My mouth tastes terrible."

Merle reaches for her purse, rummages, holds forth a peeled-down roll of mints. "Here." She pushes one into my mouth. "After your tongue is green, then we'll really kiss. Look, I'll take one too. Two green tongues, huh?"

"Merle, let me ask you. Do you remember being born?"

"Oh sure, who doesn't? I was there getting my own autograph." Her mouth is making clicking noises, the mint hitting against her teeth.

"I read about a man who claims he remembers being inside his mother's womb, and not only that, it disgusted him. He's been depressed ever since. So what do you remember?"

The mint snaps around in her mouth. "Sitting in my crib, waiting for my mother to open the door. The sun was at a nice low angle through the flowered curtains above my crib. The walls were yellow. The room was quiet and I was bored, wide awake. I watched the white door, waiting for her to come in."

Annoyed because I have no such memory, I say, "Hedy often comes home quite early from that church of hers."

Merle looks at me, her brown eyes bemused. "Tongue green yet? Stick it out, pal, stick it out!"

Having my lips bitten by a strange woman in my wife's bed. Hah!

Suddenly she sits up.

"What is it? What?"

"The front door."

"Oh, God. Never mind. Take your stuff and go into the closet. You'll be fine."

With strained dignity, Merle stares at the closet, picks up her coat and purse, crosses the room and closes herself in. I sit up. I hear nothing except a soft moan from the closet.

"Shh. What is it?"

"My gloves. I left them on the window ledge."

I have no time to reply when Hedy walks in, breathless.

"Oh, my. The church meeting was short and the drugstore was closed, so I walked over to that big new supermarket." She feels my forehead for a temperature.

"You shouldn't have walked so far after dark."

"Edna walked with me. We laughed like girls the whole way. You're feverish."

I yawn.

"Ick. Your tongue. You should see it. It's dark green!"

The unopened roll of mints sits in my hand. Hedy is reading the TV guide. "I can't make up my mind whether to take a bubble bath or come to bed. Edna's doctor told her that bubble baths cause vaginal infections. We could have a snack. I'll rub your chest and legs. Oh, tomorrow night, eight o'clock. A documentary on child abuse. In our family, we loved and obeyed our parents. They were like gods to us."

She slaps the TV guide down on the bed. "I suppose a bath would be best. No bubbles. Can I bring you something?"

"No, no. Just go off like a good dolly and run the water over your pretty body." I swat her bottom softly. I never touch her like this. I am mixing up Hedy with Merle. I am too old and weak for this sort of thing. A dying man should not engage himself in farce, romantic fluff.

The bathroom door closes. The water begins to sputter into the tub. Now I hear Hedy's flesh squeaking on the bottom of the tub. The TV. Turn it on, get noise going. The closet door opens and Merle steps out, my winter clothing a negative frame around her overnourished, bloated face.

I start to stand up, but she waves her finger no and points back to the bed. Light-headed, I sit back down, my head in my hands.

She picks up her gloves, turns down the TV, gives me a kiss on each cheek, another on the forehead. Motherly, these women are, and all of them jealous as cats. I blow a jaunty sort of kiss at her. I blow another towards her retreating rump. She closes the door and I fall back, exhausted.

✳ ✳ ✳

Half-past midnight. Propping my dizzying head in my hands, I see the bedroom door is open, a slat of light drops through from the hall. The refrigerator door is opened, shut. A drawerful of utensils is being rattled as though someone is trying to dislodge or locate something by shaking the whole mess. I hear laughter, Hedy's, Merle's . . . Good Lord.

I reach to switch on the light, then stop myself. I shall spy on them. Wrapping up in a blanket, I go over to the wedge of light and have a look. I see a peacock blue dress, then it moves farther back into the kitchen. Their voices, like gravel crushed underfoot, sound harsh, indistinct. Opening the door half an inch wider, I stick my ear into the space.

Hedy is giggling. Suppose they are talking about me, crumbling me between them like a bit of toast with their tea!

"No, I believe he's seriously ill. He has a fever, and worse, he's become odd all at once, careless of the most basic things. I can't even get him to wash. I can't even get him into the bathroom."

"But how will you get on if he kicks the bucket? Have you considered it? After my first husband punched out, I . . ."

Blood drumming in my head. Boldly discussing my death, my death! Coldhearted talk about after I am dead, what they will be eating for breakfast! And I am not even ill, only a bit out of sorts! I should march out there and show them who is still boss. Ho, there is something ghastly about two women, who should be vying for my love and financial protection, calculating their futures without me, discussing me boldly as mothers who compare their children's earaches . . . and as if I were already gone . . . not a speck of sorrow!

Women who should be enemies, boldly chatting over my weakened body. No man would do such a thing. Two men would not sit down together and chitchat about a woman. Not like that. It would be against all codes, all morals. A man's nature was to be loyal or disloyal, to obey or disobey. How else could you accomplish anything? These women float like dust, soot, silt, filth, all over the place. They have no set of rules. I can remember when I'd find a girl I liked, and bring her home, how she immediately pranced off with my sisters, while I was excluded from their stupid games and stupid confidences.

What? Have they finished speaking of me? Buried me already? Onto better things now. I go over to the bed, legs numb, head aching, try to piss into the rubber plant in the corner. After I've climbed into bed, the quilt starts to slip off but I grab with my teeth and hang on until I've managed to pull the whole thing back up.

* * *

The bedroom door opens and Hedy moves in with exaggerated quietness. Traitor, bitch. She gets into bed, smooths the blankets around us, slides over beside me. Her hand begins to move, slowly stroking my chest. My body accepts comfort; it has no pride left to it.

Hedy goes on and on, patiently stroking my chest, dragging monotonous circles with her palm against my flesh. Her hand stops its circling, comes dead center and, in conspiracy with nature, rests like the weight of the earth across my chest.

La Bête: A Figure Study

BEGINNING WITH . . .

Jeanne-Marie, an abnormally fat child of sixteen who works as a laundress at Madame Lutte's and has the afternoon off. Cook has given her a custard pie as a treat, and Jeanne-Marie has carried it all the way to the meadow outside of the village where a shallow stream runs through. She has taken off her black shoes, her black cotton stockings, and put her reddened, swollen feet into the water. Propping her elbows on her knees, she holds the pie and begins methodically to eat, her whole being occupied with the sensations in her mouth. A small splash lands in the stream near her, then another, and another. All at once she is pelted with stones that sting her neck and back. She turns, tries to get up, custard smearing her mouth, when a gang of village boys, ten or eleven years old, descend on her, grab the pie away.

"Come and get it, fatty . . ."

"Run for it, run and you can have it, here fatty, have a taste of pie."

They smash the half-pie onto the ground and surround her. She tries to push out but they are sturdy, won't let her. She cries from humiliation and that goads them further. Dragging her to

the ground, one holds her head, one her legs, while the rest unfasten her clothing until she lies there, a young, naked girl, exposed before their glinting, taunting eyes. Her primitive femaleness shocks them, then one spits and says she is a pig, a sow, a
cow. They tie up her clothes and fling them into the uppermost
branches of the tallest tree.

When they have gone, she tries to climb the tree and scratches
herself. She gives up and decides she must wait for nightfall to
return home. At the door, her father accuses her, her mother
weeps; Jeanne-Marie will tell nothing of what happened to her.
They agree she has been raped. Her father ends by thrashing her
with the hearth broom while her mother wails absurdly that she is
surely pregnant and will be a disgrace.

Jeanne puts on her blue and white striped dress, her white cotton apron, and goes out early in the morning with a long stick,
back to the meadow. She pokes at the bundle until it drops to the
ground. At Madame Lutte's house, she will spend more than
enough time scrubbing the soiled cloth of her skirt, the cloth of
her soiled blouse . . .

JEANNE-MARIE INTERRUPTS . . .

The woman stopped in our village, found me at Madame
Lutte's, scrubbing out my clothes, and asked if I would pose for a
portrait. Madame, hoping to have her own conceited self painted
for a reasonable fee, by way of ingratiating herself, let me go without protest. So, my apron still wet, I found myself seated in the
woman's carriage, driven at an eager pace to her summer chateau.

I cannot say she was unfriendly to me, but my character held
little interest for her, nor anything I might have had to say. My
figure had always brought great unhappiness to me, but here was
an artist from Paris who would find it worthy of intense, if cold

study. Into her *salon de peinture,* as she named it, with the northern window opened wide, cherry and quince blossoms jutting awkwardly from pale crocks set upon bare floors, whitewashed walls with sketches pinned here and there, she brought me. Dressed in an elegant smock of white crêpe de Chine, she asked that I remove all my clothing and mount the model's stand in the center of the room. I dropped my clothes upon a plain chair and like some ponderous creature climbed onto the model's stand. I began wringing my hands and sweating from nervousness, comforting myself with the idea of the money I was to be paid.

"Hair down. Please, unbraid your hair for me. We'll set these blossoms here, lean forward, not so much, there, fine, fine, look sideways towards me, yes, now throw the hair over one shoulder so we have the blossoms here and the hair here, yes, that's perfect. Lovely. It is essential not to move, Jeanne-Marie, until I give you permission."

My breasts hung shamelessly out before me, and my coppery hair pulled like a weight to one side of my head. The studio felt as full of warm and cold currents as a lake.

"Unbelievable laziness . . . models in Paris nowadays are utter lazybones, not wishing to strain a muscle, refusing to take positions which are too difficult."

So she talked as she worked, full of complaints, as my limbs grew heavier and heavier. I must have moved slightly, for she reprimanded me and I was afraid, and thought I would faint with fatigue.

She brought a shawl and allowed me a few minutes' rest. The immense effort of staying motionless as a chair or a dish dazed me. A platter of cold chicken and fruit was brought in, and I twisted my greasy fingers shyly through the ends of my hair and sucked the juice delicately off my fingers. When some of the violet juice dribbled down between my breasts, she told me to leave it.

After the portrait was finished, I returned to Madame Lutte's, where I quickly became discontent. I wanted to model. I quit Madame's and with this woman's references and a list of names I took a carriage to Paris, where I sought out the artists' quarters. My first employment there was so unfortunate that I nearly turned back to the life of laundress, tormented by stupid boys, in my dull country village.

The figure study class was deserted except for fifty chairs, easels, drawing boards, and the model's platform with an unlit stove near it. The russet walls were littered with caricatures and scrapings of paint from numerous palettes. I ascended the model's stand and sat in the small chair with a black fringed shawl wrapped around me. The chair bit into my thighs and I stuffed the last bit of bread I had brought into my mouth; it was dry in my mouth and I thought I could not swallow.

At last the students, all young men, herded noisily into the room. One whistled when he saw me, and joked that he must have stumbled into landscape class; he couldn't possibly be in figure study—all he saw before him was an impressive mountain of flesh.

The master arrived, establishing an air of false discipline, and asked that I assume a strange sitting posture, hands on my hips, head arched back, mouth slackly open. With a black cane, he tapped my legs apart.

Their eyes wandered over me, biting like stable flies. The studio stunk of tobacco and unwashed bodies and oil paints. I closed my eyes, imagined I was in the woman's studio with her benign eye upon me. I had no money left except what I would be paid for this day's modeling.

After an hour of brief poisonous criticisms, the master excused himself. I had taken a short break, drunk from the pitcher of water he had handed me, and now resumed my pose, my neck aching horribly from the strain. The atmosphere in the studio became loose and unrestrained. There were lighthearted denunciations of one another's work, much gossip and talk of lunch and cafés.

Unexpectedly, yet as if it were ritual, five or six of the students dragged their chairs over to the model's stand. Sitting backwards, they galloped in a circle around me, shouting obscene songs, singing the *Marseillaise,* which was forbidden by the Empire in those days. I held myself rigid, but when one of them reached up and pinched me, asking the others if they thought I could feel anything, I stood up, knocking over the slight chair, and left the studio. With enough experience, I would grow accustomed to the bizarre spirits of my art students, even playfully grabbing at the handsomer ones as they rode by me, fresh-cheeked boys on hobbyhorses. But that first day, when I complained of my treatment to the master, he asked if I would not prefer instead modeling privately for him.

This man was soon escorting me to cheap theaters, to cafés, introducing me to friends, reading from Verlaine and Baudelaire, after which he would bite my arms, muttering that I was the most delectably corpulent beast in all Paris. Sometimes he would feed me and, fascinated, watch me chew and swallow what he had placed in my mouth. I lived with him for some months, and finally prospered when he did, by a series of sketches he sold of me on brown paper.

Posing for this, for any artist, I was no longer the village freak, tormented and shunned, but was instead a figure of challenge to be studied in different positions, in varying angles of light. I was fed and given shelter in numerous garrets and studios. I wore men's clothing because it was a joke, because it was comfortable. I began to smoke tobacco and to drink wine. I laughed and no one objected, I raged and they drew out their sketchbooks. In short, the more extreme a character I displayed, the more sought after I found myself. In exchange for hams and sausage and breads, I goaded the incessant appetites of artists. I was an overnight fad in Paris, one of those meteors with a high, swift rise . . . I had become La Bête.

Not everyone liked me. One man, very fastidious, confessed that the thick petals of my flesh disgusted him, that excess such as mine revolted him. He took me one afternoon to a morgue and insisted I stare at the tables of cadavers laid out as if for some tainted feast. He explained that he had spent five years of his life drawing these gray, foul creatures.

"Look, will you, idiot! That is where someday you will be, upon a table like that one!"

I bowed and said, "And if you should arrive here before me, may I bring my knife and fork?"

At cafés among my new friends I began ordering very little food. I wished my companions to believe that La Bête ate next to nothing, that fat increased upon her like a Catholic miracle. In private, I gorged myself. I had the idea of pasting little stars of silver and gold in my red hair, and did so.

In early August I rode one evening with a group of students from the art school into the countryside. The master brought a white linen tablecloth and a pale blue oval dish with smoked salmon heaped upon it. We ended up in a meadow where the moon was bloated and discolored and the crickets howled fiendishly among the grasses. The cloth was unfolded and, shimmering like a bolt of water, was laid upon the meadow. The young men observed the effect of moonlight upon the cloth, where shadows dissolved precisely into blue edges, then white. The dish of salmon and I were asked to grace the tablecloth. I removed my trousers and shirt, put out my cigarette, and stepped upon the cloth; no one laughed or jeered at me. I had become the remarkable La Bête. Reclining in the long bed of my copper-colored hair, with the plate set before me, I took a delicate mouthful of salmon and afterward let out a long, rolling belch. Even this was accepted as art! An insult from La Bête was an occasion for art!

On the ride back to the city I bounced one of the slighter, frailer students on my lap, tickled and dandled him while the others laughed. As we came into the outskirts of an exhausted predawn Paris, I further amused them with this song:

Would you know, yes, know
How artists love? They invoke
Love with such artistry,
They are such artistic folk
That they go off saying:
Won't you come to my place,
Mademoiselle?
I'll do your portrait.

Bellowing out this last line, I added on a number of things they would do to me as I posed for their portrait.

In truth, La Bête never pretended to be chaste as a prioress. I rolled food around the cave of my mouth for pleasure and loved myself for doing so. When my father died, I returned to the village, very briefly. How small and dwarfed and without color it had become! My father as well, laid out in his stiff black suit, looked hard and yellow as the tallow soap I had used as laundress. My mother was weeping as she had been reminded to do. I despised standing in the pitiful cemetery of my ancestors. I loathed the villagers, staring as if I were still their own fat Jeanne-Marie, and not a famous Impressionist's model.

One night I modeled in the great Parisian cemetery for a group of male students and two of their girls. One foot I planted upon the small raised headstone of a child and one hand I held behind my head. My hair, braided over my breasts, glittered with stars. As I held the position, my muscles growing numb from strain, I felt a sticky, filmy sensation slide down my inner thigh. I brought my finger down, lifted it to the moon, and exposed, oily and black as paint, my glistening flux. My blood left bright banners upon the child's headstone. The little stone would be discolored, ruined, in the daylight, and my boys thought it a perfect omen of some sort, though they did not know of what.

HOW JEANNE-MARIE MAY HAVE SOUNDED AS LA BÊTE:

. . . to be thin is to be subject to an invasion of the ordinary. When I eat, I try always to be alone. I rarely use a plate. Dishes are mediators, and cups, interferences with the directness of a bottle. I do use a bowl for my soup. I keep myself as well stocked as a cook's cupboard. Artists wallow their brushes in paint and swish, slop, make for themselves a gloriously fat beast. Me.

What I have never been able to do is to take joy in my bulk. Back in my village I was taught it was wicked to take up so much room, so when I watch these artists take their peculiar joy in me, in those moments, I feel good.

People wonder what it's like to make love to a fat woman. In the way people like to use something half up and then discard it, so a fat one like myself is used up. Or perhaps a man merely wishes to debase himself. Or become an infant against his mamma.

The latest man, this silly artist, he presses the juices from me. He says the water overflows the jug and I am the jug. I have posed over three weeks in this same attitude, stepping out from a tub, my buttocks toward him, my eyes looking straight into the bathtub. Yes, there's a little scum of water in it, stale as any water that sits. He waits until the light comes through the windows at the correct exposure, heaves a bucket of water over me, orders me to step into the tub, then feverishly rushes back to his easel. He has me hold until my ass trembles from the effort to be still.

Sometimes, with my one foot splayed out in the water, I begin to sing bawdy verses to pique him. On occasion I fart and say, "Put that onto your canvas, you fool!" This man is very famous, not used to insult, so I am glad to give it.

I sit on the edge of the tub or lie on the bed to smoke one of the cigarettes I've rolled for myself. Funny, this one tells me that I have grace. My flesh is full of lights, he says. Nothing about me disgusts him. He goes outside while I eat my meal of sausage and cold potato; he returns in exactly five minutes.

Do I care anymore what they put on the canvas? Not much. I come over and blow smoke at the buttocks he has drawn and daubs with greenish-white.

"What horse apples," I snort and go, breathlessly, back to the bathtub.

Peculiar man. He likes to paint my huge bulk in erotic common postures, yet he never approaches me except with the bucket of water, then stabs in queer, caressing ways at the canvas with his brushes!

He calls me his mule, heaving the damn water over me, making me hunch for hours over this cracked porcelain until I cry out. Remorseful, he apologizes by throwing sausage and bread at me and turning his back.

I tear into the meat, huge mouthfuls, my pubic hair staring up at me, a reproachful orange mouth. When the picture is finished, I am given money, and I stare hard at the painting.

"Well, my mule, what do you think? It's perfect, is it not?"

"It stinks," I say, and he never hires me again.

DESCENT OF LA BÊTE . . .

Oh, when was it that my boys, my creators, began to neglect me? They lost their imaginations, that's what, sneaking into their garrets and studios such ordinary, slender grisettes . . . I tore up one lover's drawings during the night he did not return home. He went off with a bony nag who did nothing but crochet from her little basket and snub me. My temper grew worse; not one had the courage or the patience to risk using me. One newly arrived painter who had no money but offered to share his food used me, and I violently attacked his work, saying, "You call this a work of art?"

"And you," he screamed back, sweeping his pastels off the table onto the floor, "do you call yourself a work of nature—you are one of her aberrations!"

I abandoned that young fool in the middle of his work.

They had no more use for me, they could find no more art in me. Acquaintances in cafés vanished, or turned away their faces, and miserable La Bête came at last to selling flowers and matches on the hard steps of the Luxembourg, though she kept stars in her hair, as always.

One morning I sold more than enough flowers to pay my way into the museum. I moved through a hushed, churchlike maze of pictures and busts, until I found myself . . . enormously fat and red with a small head, reclining in a wet, blurred orchard like some rotting, overripe fruit. I had been uncovered like this, before the world, and now they had no more use for me. I sat on the floor and wept and beat my fists upon the floor, tried to scratch the picture, until two, then three guards took me out. I told them who I was and as I was pushed out I spat into the fountain, hoping to pollute the false, fickle waters of art.

But the sickness never left me. I needed them, however much I disliked their results. Creeping back to the ateliers, I asked, then begged for work. I reformed my temper, but my poor health . . . I had begun with little fits of sleep, narcolepsy. On the model's stand, not even a poor student wanted me. La Bête was broken-winded.

LA BÊTE AND THE RECLUSE

An endless monotony of rain ran off the black slate roofs. It was gray and chill as only Paris can be in October, when even bread is damp. It became too cold to sit on the museum steps any longer.

Oh, sweet fall of the rain
Upon the earth and roof
Unto a heart in pain,
O music of the rain.

The houseboat was tied up beside others of its type, broken down, peeling, bleached, ruined. I knocked, opened the small red door, and went in sideways.

"No, I have little need of a model like yourself. I have no need of anyone or anything but paint and God."

He was willfully blind to anything outside his tiny, cramped houseboat. Boxes, papers, broken furniture, garbage stacked to the ceiling, narrow snakelike paths from his bed to his easel, from his easel to his stove. He stank vilely, but insisted that his layers of clothing ventilated him. And his canvases, strewn about like blowing litter on a street, some propped up, others lying face down, to ripen with the movement of the water, he said. He painted me standing in the middle of a salmon-colored river with black skies. He painted me wading in a choppy cobalt sea with no features on my face. I cleared away some of his boxes and furniture to make a bed for myself and a small toilette. I cooked on his small filthy stove, but since he often neglected to eat I learned to eat his portion before it grew cold. I smoked outside and regarded the ramshackle wharf. Odd, that an artist for whom only beauty mattered would choose such grim clutter.

We suffered that winter; snow drifted through unclosed windows. I found two cheap rooms in Paris and we left the houseboat. Strange to be in open, ill-favored space with this man. Wallpaper dangling in faded, defeated strips, plaster crumbling off the ceiling. The view from our two windows was of a tiny stamp of courtyard with arthritic burls of chestnut trees staring indifferently back at us.

His paintings were washed in half-light, phosphorescent, devoid of sunlight. He was a creature of dampness and night and perverse conversations. There was a benefactor who infrequently purchased his paintings, and on this, but mainly on donation, we existed.

When he became unwell, medicines made their way into our rooms, and the place where he slept was blatant with suggestions of a sickroom: a spoon in a tumbler of clouded water, a mortar and pestle, packets of white powder, stained rags by the pillows. A cat lived with us, an old calico who sat in his lap when he dozed upright in a chair. Late in the spring he began complaining of cold and went about in a shabby brown fur-lined overcoat, a white nightshirt, and black trousers, with a short black coat over all this.

We had enough money from the sale of a painting to hire a carriage for an evening's ride into the country. My friend was in some nocturnal reverie, walking through groves of birch, stepping across streambeds, leaning against a small limestone cliff, while I cursed and swore, trying to keep up with him. I also remembered the glorious night when I had been a feast of inspiration for young artists, reclined upon a white tablecloth.

He painted my head, took it off with the palette knife, began a second time, allowed it to dry, scraped again, in this way building up form, refining the drawing; after each scraping there would be a subtle layer of paint left. Being too feverish to go and purchase proper paint, at one point he seized the candle off its dish and used the grease from it to paint with. Fasting and improvised prayers over his work went on hour after hour. He had no use for my once-famous body, painting only my head, with a green scarf concealing my famous hair, tobacco smoke like a fine, hissing aureole around me. I was to be laughing, some of my teeth missing, my cheeks mapped with broken veins. But the sitting went badly. I kept dropping off to sleep, and he was exhausted, able to work for only a quarter of an hour at a time.

The cat would hunch upon a broken arm of a couch, delicately washing itself. We worked only at night, the glowing tongues of many lamps and candles wagging wastefully around us.

He told me, "In darkness the trivial is unwelcome. In an absence of light, first the face, then the shadows around the face."

I grunted, half-asleep.

"So it is among common people that you will find grace."

I woke up. "Oh, crap. Common people fling rocks at the backs of common people." I coughed and spat phlegm onto the floor. "You call that grace, you idiot, you beloved idiot of mine?"

"Oh, yes," he said, his eyes on mine like a priest's.

When I awoke from another of my sick little naps, the lamps and candles guttered weakly in the morning sunlight, and I found my artist, who needed nothing but God and paint and me to cook for him, me to grind up his medicines for him, me to sit for him, had gone, his head fallen over into the wet oils of my open-mouthed portrait.

Looking as if he had fed himself to the devil.

La Bête had devoured him, it seemed.

AS IT TURNS OUT . . .

After feeding and bathing her mother, Jeanne-Marie walks to the other end of the village, where old Madame Lutte still lives. In her basket she has rolled up the white cloth from Paris. When she gets inside the laundry room lined with its dark, cool stone, she fills the metal tubs, one with hot water, the other with cool. Disregarding the baskets of soiled linens and dresses, Jeanne-Marie takes out the white cloth, feeds it into the steaming water, takes the tallow bar of soap, and begins scrubbing. Her hands work among the cloth and the water, like red fish they move, quick and chapped. The cool water accepts the cloth, and a grayish scum of soap rings the metal tub. Wringing out the tablecloth, she stretches it across a rope to dry in the summer sunlight. It floats, a square unnatural cloud, against the blue seamless heaven.

Jeanne-Marie returns to the laundry room, pours out the fouled water, and begins the tedious, ordinary job of washing out Madame Lutte's expensive dresses and linens.

By noon the tablecloth is hanging stiffly across the rope, smelling of sunlight, and Jeanne-Marie's work is finished. She rolls the cloth into her basket along with the cold joint of meat and slice of cake given her by the cook.

In the familiar patch of meadow, she shakes out the snowy tablecloth, sets down the plate of meat and pie. Removing her blue and white striped dress, her apron, her heavy shoes and black stockings, Jeanne-Marie sits crosslegged upon the cloth, unbraiding her hair until it drops in a coppery sheet around her.

The poplar trees at the edge of the meadow clamor and flash silver in the strong afternoon breeze. She chews, sensuously and deliberately, wiping her fingers in her hair. Abruptly, she drops into sleep; the sun bleaches out her flanks, sets dull fire to her hair, sparkles against the sharp-edged white cloth in the sour grasses.

The village boys peer through a particularly dense stand of poplar trees; having discovered the habits of this queer laundress, they have snuck out from their chores to ogle her, in a kind of nervous dread of her enormity. There is something of an ogress in her raw pose, something of a folktale in the way her huge fans of flesh lie open before them. Their fathers and mothers only know Jeanne-Marie as Madame Lutte's ugly, disgraced laundress, in her shabby dress with her red chafed hands and broken chatter. But these boys know the awful enchantment of her naked body, set out as if for a feast upon an immaculate white square in the sunny meadow.

La Bête, even asleep, feels the boys out there, their pale, un-ripened faces shifting among the green leaves, their whispers like a shaking of wind through the poplars. She allows them, for she is worthy of study. Her figure commands attention. La Bête knows that her boys, her artists, can never have enough of her. She is that good.

The Housekeeper

The Reverend felt his housekeeper's fingers tapping a senseless braille against his pajamas. Why did he allow her to awaken him like this? Her face, grooved and flat as a gas pedal, looked down at his. He grimaced up to signal he was awake and rolled over. Satisfied, Mrs. Gump limped to the window. Grasping the cord by its plastic bell, she jerked back the curtains.

The Reverend pitched over again and lay back, helpless as an invalid under her peevish ritual, waiting for her to go before he could turn back the bedspread and set his feet on the floor. But she stood steady as a flagpole, her maroon kimono with its iridescent green dragonflies pinned around her. What was keeping her? The Reverend sat up cautiously. She was peering out the window, her lip jutting in and out like a pump. With a prophetic face, she turned to him.

"What is it, Mrs. Gump?"

She rolled her eyes until they seemed to disappear like dark pits into her face.

"Storm, Holy Reverend."

"Oh."

He was distinctly not interested in the variations of the weather. Didn't one day trot along like the next, until Sunday, when everyone turned to him for reassurance? He had given up trying to introduce God into every home. It would be far easier to stride into a house with a vacuum to demonstrate than to sidle in, as he did, a Bible weighing apologetically in his left hand. Sensible people, he had learned, never welcomed past their doorstep what they couldn't try out in plain light. So the Reverend kept out of harm's way. He invented sermons, buried, baptized, and married, quietly and without fuss. He was a shadow, easy to turn from, always retrievable, and a persistent reminder of where everyone was headed.

There were those, like Mrs. Gump, who treated him with fanatical esteem, jealous of his position, critical of his person. She took fastidious pains with the equipment of his office. His vestments could stand upright in the pulpit, made independent of him by her weekly starchings. Yet his bed linen was rumpled and gray-tinged, his house stale and littered with half-used cleaning products. The food she laid out for him was execrable, yet the Reverend, reminding himself of the world's poor, could not bring himself to request anything better. Mrs. Gump, when she went shopping on Mondays and visiting on Thursdays, swung her head dolefully over his fog-headedness, while he approached his spotless paper and polished texts with his neglected person, convinced that virtue, that workhorse of faith, lay in doing whatever one most disliked.

Mrs. Gump spat into the empty flower pot by the back steps. Scrub up with a lye-soaked brush, and grime would worm its way into the slits of your knuckles anyway. She knew a person could kneel day and night before the Lord, but the instant he was on his feet, he would be back amongst the unclean.

"I'll spit whenever it pleases me to do so. They'll tote me under the dirt soon enough. My soul's clean."

Mrs. Gump squatted in her black dress on the back steps, rolling the handle of the broom up and down her bony lap, squinting across the yard at the yellow irises by the chain-link fence. Beauty provoked her. She owned none of its properties. It was unclear to her what beauty had to do with fearing the Lord and living clean. Cleanliness was what she was paid for, but as much as she claimed to be soaping and rinsing and wiping down and brushing into a rubber dustpan, a steady sour track of deterioration followed her about the house. Mrs. Gump stalked the spoor of dirt through square rooms and down sidewalks and around the rims of trees and pots and toilet bowls. If she stood still long enough, dust would descend and cover her. If she stood still long enough, which she refused to do, everything in back of her and to the sides of her would unloose, or else everything that was supposed to be straight would ravel and loop up. In a holy fit, she whacked six of the week's days into order with a homemade broom, and the seventh she pressed like a tobacco leaf between the cool, monument-like pages of her Bible. She stumped through each pagan day with the sparse ferocity of a prophet, pumping her lip in and out, her hair spiked into a boil at the nape of her neck. And on Sunday mornings she sat rigid in the front pew, proud that this man was dependent on her for his daily support.

Mrs. Gump gnawed the orange handle of her broom and sniffed the air like a querulous dog. She turned her head west. She knew when a storm of some proportion was coming long before anyone else, and she anticipated doomsday with the confidence shared by the morbid and the righteous.

"Purge, scour, disinfect, and rub raw," she muttered, standing up and swiping at the gray warped steps with the broom.

"Descend this minute, hose us down. Rid us of all unclean and vain things."

She scowled a last time at the unpleasant yellow irises before going back inside to wash her hands and rinse off the stains of vision before setting hand to the minister's food.

I was fortunate. I began by painting houses, but now I pin the quick faces of villagers to pieces of canvas. The face of the Reverend leans against a window, selfish and drying. Some faces reject light. I am blessed because there are a sad lot of people in this world who begin sketching portraits and finish by swaying on scaffolding, slapping shingles gray and clapboards white, stucco scraping them like barnacles. I have painted the face of everyone in this village. I would call that a kind of ownership.

When I had finished painting the outsides of their houses and was well paid, I stepped politely inside. Each adult and child above the age of four sat in a ladder-back chair by an east window, restrained as an overnight guest, while I overlooked their individual falseness and set their unholy histories as close to the pure surface of the canvas as I could. I imagine they would sit before God like that, trying to look as blameless as possible. At noon I would lie between rows of bulging-headed cabbages in the victory garden and transport my town, in the form of simple square paintings, to a museum. Now, when I am terribly inspired or overcome by heat, I consider beginning over, returning to the houses and making second portraits of everyone in order to compare the effect of time and decay upon the first. Or I consider slyly painting the back of the head, like sensing the passage toward noon through the warm surface of a stone. It can be done.

Portraits, even badly done, are flattering, and people distrustful, so I began innocently enough, with their houses, then with their oval prairie-stamped faces, scraping them clean, starting fresh, in competition with their original maker.

I have, on occasion, desired to paint limbs and torsos, more poignant perhaps than faces . . . the dark arrow between the legs pointing upward to the buttocks, or the lines binding the neck like butcher's string around a roast. No one has asked me to teach, to admit that there are techniques and ways of abusing technique. There is no one to admire what I am capable of. You know, people here are proud of their silly portraits. They mount them shyly amid the ceramic bric-a-brac, the chipped swan-necked vases. The druggist hung his face beside his clock, the dentist displays his in the waiting room above the magazine rack, and the man who runs the small gas station and grocery moves his every few days, so flies don't walk across it, he says.

Mrs. Gump, my apologies. I have not gone near your face yet. Your face, unsparing as a line from the Old Testament, flat as the bottom of a funeral urn, will be my final test. But you will not want your portrait, nor would the minister care for another of you, and I doubt that I would want you, as my own mother, struggling to spit just as I am shaping and freezing your lips.

Incidentally, I have observed how absence enhances the color of remembered objects and how proximity diminishes all things. The painting recalled is brilliant in texture and theme, the one recently laid aside, insipid, dull. I am sure of it, as I am sure each life imitates this general scheme. So please, understand why I paint. Rebelling against the larger background of creation and destruction, in which I had no choice and was not consulted, I sit, hunched and full of aches, my brush in angry, skilled revolt.

The Reverend set down his slender pen and picked up the receiver of the telephone after the second ring. To wait until the second ring made him seem less anxious for company. He placed the black piece against his ear and with his free hand nudged his glasses up until they settled and glinted ceilingward. In a neutral tone he answered, "Good morning, this is the Reverend . . ."

What he heard in response was not a voice, but wind. It was exactly like hearing the ocean in a shell cupped to his ear. However, in this case he heard not water but wind. He sat there, holding the phone, fascinated. The sound he heard was not pure. It was dull, gritty, and belligerent. This was not the sound of a cleansing, restorative breeze, but a sound littered with complaint. Gingerly he dropped the receiver onto the telephone and creaked around in his armchair to look out the window. The air was quivering as if it had been slapped. It was also yellow. The Reverend replaced his glasses over his weak eyes and turned to read the last sentence he had written on his legal tablet. He was writing, again, about charity beginning at home. He was adept at buttoning up the same theme in a whole line of cheap suits, an ability which he did not consider dishonest, simply economical. To be a mouth-piece for the divine demanded neither creativity nor courage, only memory and a good ear. The experience of the wind in the telephone disturbed him. He got up and left his study, his incomplete sermon, to walk out into his garden.

Mrs. Gump stood at the iron clawfooted sink, squeaking up her wet hands with Fels Naptha. He was hoping he could step past her unremarked, an unlikely prospect. She had both the instincts and profile of a badger.

"That you, Holy Reverend?"

"Yes, it is," he answered overbrightly, laying his hand to the screen door. As he did, she snapped off the faucets.

"Storm's moving close." She wiped her hands down her dress. The pipes shuddered.

His housekeeper took excessive pride in her predictions. She enjoyed whatever favor the Lord chose to cast over her for the education of others. Whereas he, an ordained man of God, moved among the thin shadows of his dilapidated church, not thinking to raise his head or his speculations much higher than the broken bell tower. Preaching, burying, baptizing, he did not have time to sort out his relationship with his employer in any personal way. This demonstrated, he thought cynically and unfairly, the profound gulf between them. Faith was a hobby on her part, something akin to gluing sequins on soda bottles, and a sober, responsible profession on his.

She stood there facing him, skinny yellow arms braced at the sink, in her black dress, pleased with herself. Would he have to see her in heaven as well?

"Those flowers of yours . . ." She lowered her eyes and intoned solemnly, "Might need some staking if you want them to beat out the storm."

He looked out the screen door at the irises. The air had become dull and still, yet the bright flowers seemed to be in perpetual subtle motion. Nodding and not looking at her, he stepped out.

"Lunch will be served sometime or other in the next hour. Fried chicken," she called out after him.

"Lunch," he snorted to himself once he was safely out of earshot. What half-baked bird, unreconciled to the shock of its own murder, would be slapped down on the table and expected to shore up his dwindling flesh—ha!—he could imagine.

The Reverend took deep pleasure in his backyard garden, though he had done nothing to encourage its existence. Four years earlier the town's Garden and History Club had swept through the town, beautifying and memorializing, and had stopped with stricken looks in front of the minister's house. His yard was scraped and bare and shameful. With his bemused permission, they tunneled like moles, digging, spading, pointed straw hats with turquoise nets covering their sweating faces, inserting bulbs, tubers, roots, and spraying seed with a delicate flip of the fingers across the reluctant soil. Before they left, in a complacent sighing gaggle, they instructed the Reverend, with the seriousness of surgeons, to water the entire yard with one inch of water per week, information which he passed on to Mrs. Gump and which she passed on to the blackest corridor of her intentions, so that the yard received only an occasional bitter dousing from Mrs. Gump in her wrinkled plaid sunbonnet, an occasional harried drowning from the Reverend, and a few chance freakish rainfalls. After several seasons of gross neglect and mismanagement, the hardier species endured and even appeared to flourish. The yard was choked with blue carpet bugle, yellow iris, and a common variety of sedum, the leaves of which resembled butter lettuce and felt to the touch like clusters of damp earlobes.

The Reverend veered out to the clump of irises and stood with his hands behind his back, gazing down into their fleshy throats, admiring their audacity. To think they would display their sexual organs so showily, to actually be cultivated for the color and arrangement of one's genitals. He imagined, for an unholy moment, the people of the town planted like this, heads submerged like bulbs, and genitals flowerlike, moist, and rosy, exposed to the wind and the astonishment of passersby. He shook his head clear. Not at all, by any stretch, a pretty speculation.

He suddenly felt the wind climb up from the lawn beneath him. It seemed to eddy around his feet, then sail up his ankles. His trousers flapped wildly around his stemlike legs, then lay molded against them, unresisting. He looked up and saw that his perception had been inaccurate. The wind, Mrs. Gump's prediction, was overtaking everything at once. He turned toward the house and saw Mrs. Gump behind the screen door, watching him. He must appear blurred, waterish, beside his blowing irises. He was in the midst of the shell sound he had heard over the telephone. Mrs. Gump opened the door against the force of the blowing dust and debris and yelled something to him which he could not hear. Then he saw her motion, her arm like a crank, to come inside. But he could imagine the satisfied expression on her face because the irises were being shredded and bruised by the stinging dust. There would be troughs of pleasure around her eyes because the irises were bent down, because beauty was marred by death. She would seize upon the implication of divine justice. Stubbornly, he turned and headed for the garage. He emerged with string and stakes, ignoring Mrs. Gump's frantic gestures to come inside. Kneeling into the wind, his eyes sealed half shut by the dust which discolored the plants and obscured the air, he clumsily poked the stakes into the ground and lashed the irises to them so that they stood like fat green and yellow bundles. As he straightened up and made his way back to the house, he noted with satisfaction that his housekeeper had not stayed to watch.

The storm had settled on a monotonous pitch. Dust suffocated the leaves, sprayed the ground and the fences a putty color. Fastening the door shut, the Reverend noticed a spray of dust across the linoleum and a lunular shaped arc of it on the red table. He crossed to the window which Mrs. Gump had left gaping, shut and locked it. The chicken in the frying pan was cut up and coated in flour and dust. He turned off the flame beneath it. He thought he should go throughout the house and seal the windows and cracks and spaces. He felt exhilarated, boyish. My house is a wooden vessel, pitching and riding the billows of dust. But, he sighed, as he blew dust from the table onto the floor, a dismal crew. Dismal.

At that moment he heard Mrs. Gump hissing damply. She sounded like a camel he had once observed, molting and chained up in a traveling zoo. Her eyes, he saw as he peeked around the door of the kitchen, were beveled with rage, her bottom lip stuck out like a cheap shard. As he watched, she raised her fists to heaven as though she were gripping a baseball bat and prayed loudly, spontaneously, in a wild-sounding gibberish.

The artist leaned against the wall with a pained and tense smile across the lower third of his face. Such a smile was his only reaction to his mother's abusive curses. She hurled her memorized bits of the Bible at him, and he stood with rotten scriptural fruit on his face, with holy refuse clotting his otherwise plain clothing. She resembled, he decided, an Italian gargoyle set up, barking, to guard the dingy premises. Then he saw the Reverend, gray with dust, and, ignoring his idiotic mother, flourished the package in the air, causing dust to shake down in a cloud about his figure.

"It's done," he shouted, "finished!"

The housekeeper spat disgustedly onto the floor by the artist's feet and limped away, down the hall which was dark and narrow as a cervix, while the Reverend stepped out and embraced the artist whom he had not seen for several weeks.

In the near background he heard Mrs. Gump scaling the vertical slopes of the porch with her vacuum. An appropriate time to

clean, he observed. Dust sifting all around them in opaque, choking light. The windows were clamped down, the doors shut . . .
the doorsills were jammed with balls of newspaper and folded
magazines. But here it was, a fine chalklike powder, whitening
everything. He rolled a small mouthful of red wine around in his
mouth. His earlier spurt of excitement had wound down into
lethargy. His conversation with the artist had defaulted into the
artist's muffled and indistinct monologue. He had already heard
the elm trees in his front yard described as outflung legs of brown
corduroy. The Reverend marveled at the artist's capacity to associ-
ate perfect incongruities. Corduroy and tree bark, for instance.
Although, given a moment's free thought, he too saw the sense of
it. Fabric for skin, bark was fabric for treeflesh. Yes, of course. It
wasn't so difficult. He stared with admiration at the artist, someone who could entertain himself while the room broke to bits
around him. Of course the Reverend had his spells of imagining.
Every educated person did. But he considered it in the interests of
maintaining a modest profile to suppress these imaginings, to nip
them in their buds, as it were. But this man, this artist with the
broad lentiginous hands, he let the world sift through his fingers
as though it were all wreckage and it was his job to reclaim and re-
create. The minister tried to make sense of the world to his con-
gregation, to be simple, to repeat the simple themes. This other
man, the artist, made a hash of the world, burst it apart with a
crack from his hand. He reveled in disorder out of which he cre-
ated his own particular world, perfectly cold, perfectly self-sus-
taining, as indifferent to the needs of the flock as nature herself.
Mrs. Gump had always maintained that her son was corrupt, and
for a strained moment the Reverend saw her point. But he shared
something with the artist. He couldn't place a name for it, but it
made him one step closer to the artist and one step farther from
Mrs. Gump.

He was tempted to lift the receiver and listen to the wind. But
he did not. Gradually he grew aware that the artist had given up
speech and was sitting still, watching everything about him. The
muffled roar of the vacuum had cut off as well. The wind was

tossing the three of them silently about. Fine silt enshrouded them. They were being linked by wind and by dust. Outside, the street was sunken in dust, everything had fallen beneath the dun, scabbish texture of a street mongrel.

As he talked, the artist leaned out from his chair, rubbing dust off the lip of the bottle with one short, spattered finger. He rubbed faster, pressing until his fingertip whitened and the green glass whined. The Reverend winced, the artist apologized. Laughing, he lifted up the bottle to pour himself and the Reverend more of the wine he had brought along.

The Reverend sat in his chair, his feet propped on the desk top. The artist sat to his left, in the visitor's chair, his feet also resting on the desk. Their shoes nearly met at the heels; the artist's paint-speckled workboots covered his feet like bloated dark sausages. The Reverend wore his blue felt house slippers with the gold fleur-de-lis pattern. His slippers, with his white feet emerging from them like roots, rested heavily on the yellow legal tablet which he noticed the artist glancing at with a childish greed that was embarrassing. In an attempt at privacy, he kept his feet crossed and planted right over his algebraic-looking script. This required effort, as he had kept good pace with the artist's furious drinking, and his legs felt heavy as sewer pipes, and his head seemed eternally riveted on the window behind the artist's head. The portrait of himself, inaccurate in every detail, yet not unflattering and somewhat inspired, was propped beneath the window. The flat-featured Reverend looked into the room, breathing in the light. The other Reverend looked out the window, intrigued by the theatrical tricks of the storm.

The artist, his tongue both thickened and loosened by wine, was rooting noisily among heaps of imagery at top speed. The Reverend counted two sparrows slamming clumsily into the glass, and a menu blew by which he recognized as belonging to his neighbor's café. A Rhode Island Red hen sailed by backwards, puffed and indignant. The storm was making a mockery of the village. He watched a garden hat with a turquoise veil bang against the window and then be tilted high up and away. Was this a random selection of things being destroyed and displaced? This brought him to the idea of predestination, of which he was frightened and therefore believed in.

The telephone rang once. The artist set his glass on the blotter of the desk and started to ask for paper. At that moment Mrs. Gump limped down the hall and stood slack as a hooked fish in the doorway. Her hair swung in filthy disarray around her shoulders. Her breasts and midriff flopped like chamois pouches under the dusty dress. In the doorway where she stood, it appeared to both the artist and the Reverend that she was crying.

The artist stared down into his empty glass, afraid, for the first time, of the way her joints sagged from their sockets like balls of rotten string. He suddenly felt that her defeat would diminish him. He had painted the village to prove to her that the village could be painted. He drew portraits to show her that faces could be captured. He had proved to her that God was not the only Creator, and her curses were proof to him that he had succeeded. He might have no reason to paint if she were dead.

The Reverend stared, openmouthed, at her. He experienced an aberrant desire to lay her down on the eye-shaped rug with the trumpet lilies twined on it, so that he could lose his hands under her flag-stiff fabric. But his lust, he realized, was not for her body, not for her flesh, but for her signs of holiness. She had accomplished, to him, the most difficult thing. She had given up the temptation of being loved in this world, of loving this world, so that she could be loved and cherished in the next. He had wavered, unfixed, had lain low while she had never ceased believing. Now he coveted her faith with the bitter hunger of the uncommitted.

"Shower head's broke off. There's water on the tiles . . ."

Her face was wet from attempting to fix the plumbing. The artist looked relieved, and the Reverend sat up straight, looking grave and dignified.

Mrs. Gump groped her way through the choking dust over to

the window, to watch the pieces of the town, like a disassembled puzzle, blow past her. Everything was being unfastened from daily usage, released from common meaning.

She heard, after a time, their pencils against the paper. One writing. One drawing. She saw little difference between lines which made a face and shapes which formed a word.

She would put a stop to the foolishness of the world. Pumping her lip in and out, she drew shut the curtains with a snap. For the few seconds that the room was hers, utterly dark and thick with dust, she prayed aloud and triumphant. But when the light switched on over the Reverend's desk and the two of them went on calmly working, tying themselves to life even as it covered them over with dust, her voice failed.

She was only, after all, the housekeeper.

Taking Hold of Renee

Twelve wives poke about the island cemetery, reading aloud the more tragic inscriptions.

Things must decay like mad in this heat and humidity! This from the young woman nearest Renee, the one closest in age to herself. Oooh, here's a saddy, Susanna Wicklow, two small sons and a husband aged twenty-nine, "all bleffedly removed from earth's mortal gloom," May 1789. Those poor British must have sailed over and dropped like flies.

With a trained decorum reminiscent of the schoolgirls they had all once been, the wives file into the stone church.

No one can locate Renee until a search finds her sitting on the ground within one of the churchyard's numerous hedged enclosures, her head like a flower, tipped heavily on her folded arms. It is an unkempt space, a place where dead leaves and broken branches are thrown, a sort of compost heap, is what the wives think, until they notice the little limestone hump beside Renee. The size marker used for a child.

A tactful retreat, so that the women, many of them grand-mothers, can reconfirm the story of Renee's little girl, kidnapped less than two years ago, found dead in a forest preserve near the parents' home. Brisk cheerfulness is agreed upon, to behave as if unintimidated by such leviathan tragedy.

Renee dear, we thought we'd lost you! Some of the others have gone on to the shops before we meet husbands for lunch; the rest are heading to the little post office for stamps. Come with us, won't you?

* * *

Her skin glints, mother of pearl. Renee puts on her new red bathing suit, her limbs poking out from it like white eels. Her stomach never really flattened after Emily's birth. Her body's whiteness is an embarrassment. Like someone whose one over-prominent feature upstages the rest, Renee feels singled out by her skin. She looks freakish against the fiery green tropical back-drop, a specter beside the natives. She had watched, along with the other wives, when a black man in a red nylon bikini, his shoul-der-length hair braided into dozens of wiry snakes, sprinted along the beach before diving elegantly into the sea. Now that's a jungle bunny, isn't it? one of the women said. I think he looks wonder-ful, Renee said distinctly, and the women looked at her with curiosity.

* * *

The librarian had suggested *Wide Sargasso Sea* for a trip to the West Indies, but Renee finds the novel risky, about a nineteenth-century Creole heiress going piecemeal mad amid the oozy decay and red bloom of the tropics. It reads too much like a more lyric version of her own concealed voice:

"I never looked at any strange negro. They hated us. They called us white cockroaches. Let sleeping dogs lie. One day a little girl followed me singing, 'Go away white cockroach, go away, go away.' I walked fast, but she walked faster. 'White cockroach, go away, go away. Nobody wants you. Go away.'"

Renee reexamines this passage. Is this what they think of us? She looks at the other women in the chaise longues, piled around her like reddening seals on rocks. The bolder few of their group are out snorkeling, their rented black tubes finning across the slightly peaky water. She shifts uncomfortably in her own chair, her limbs exposed and pale.

On her way back to the room to change for cocktails and dinner, Renee stops at one of the outdoor showers near the beach. Black birds with lemony eyes and doves the color of washed blood group in the coarse, choppy grass, waiting to bathe in her water.

Renee picks her way, guiltily, past uniformed employees on the curving paths bordered with yellow hibiscus and purple bougainvillea. Their taxi driver had said that over one quarter of the island men were without work except during sugar cane harvests. Security guards patrol their resort. Waiters are college graduates who move, dispirited, from table to table. The island, dependent on tourism and foreign investment, has, like most dependent entities, repressed hostility until it emerges as unctuous inefficiency. The majority of people live, poorly clothed, in cramped wooden shacks with no running water.

* * *

Nights, after rum punch and candlelit dinners by the sea, after sotted, jolly sing-a-longs ("Yellow Bird," "Down the Way Where the Nights Are Gay"), nights are the worst for them. Since Emily's murder, Renee rejects pleasure. Her mourning is vigilant, extended; she hates the weakness in Bill's character which argues for intimacy. Sex would be a selfish abandonment of Emily. Renee's ascetic grief, the sterility it imposes on them, ill suits the seductive tropics.

They have quarreled over this, Bill painfully asking that Renee seek counseling when they return home, Renee countering that he betrays their daughter, doesn't he, by so quickly expecting that she resume some normal life.

* * *

On their last day the group rides in open jeeps to a restaurant for breakfast. Tables have been lined up along a flowered terrace overlooking the Caribbean. Some of the wives deftly focus cameras, pressing about an ornate black cage recessed into a grotto near a fountain sloppy with brackish water. The frilly cage holds a green monkey. After the others go to their seats, Renee stays, sitting on the cool rock ledge beside the cage. The monkey, hyperalert, is fuzzed much like a coconut, its fur greenish yellow like woodland moss. Tree ferns submerge its cage in watery emerald light. On the bottom of the cage is a life-sized baby, face down, in a torn pink shift spattered with watermelon seeds. One of the doll's arms is missing, its hair is in dirty blond screw-curls. The monkey thrusts its sinewy arm through the cage bars, touches Renee on the shoulder. Renee lets it hold her hand, its finger pads black, slick ovals . . . it seizes at her head, feathering through her long red hair with eerily intelligent fingers. Renee wants to sit forever near the monkey, never leave the broken baby at bottom, near the lip of muddy rainwater.

Later she tucks most of her breakfast into a napkin, hides it in the swallow of her purse, and feeds the fuzzed, parted mouth of the green monkey. Bill comes back from the parking lot, his face anxious, resentful. Please, Renee, everyone's waiting for you. Let's try, shall we? Today's our last day . . .

* * *

Renee has been gulping wine, eating a little bread, trapped at the dinner table again. Bill is asking the other young wife in their group what, in her opinion, gives a man sex appeal. He is a little drunk, she sees, and veering out of context. Next he stands, offers a gregarious, inclusive toast. A college education is mostly bunk, he begins, if you want to get into business and succeed, which— he gestures broadly—I seem to have done.

God, she thinks, he is that simple, content with himself, he suffers, recovers, goes on. Perhaps that is his gift, a certain overlooking of messy, unresolving grief. No slowing the machinery, no affecting the process. And he can still trust life; Renee almost envies him that.

After dinner Bill dances with the wife who had answered without a hitch that what makes a man sexy are two things—good eyes and great buns. Renee wonders if it is gratitude she should feel toward this woman dancing quite close to Bill, then feels as if she is suffocating.

* * *

Running from the party, the dancing, Renee drops her sandals at the edge of the manicured, torchlit lawn. Runs along the flat beach toward the fishing village, above which the moon lists, an apricot bulge. She nearly trips over a man squatting beneath a manchineel tree, cooking fish over a low fire. Runs by a man bathing himself in one of the resort's outdoor showers, rubbing soap over himself with furtive, quick slides of his hand. The sea is tearing up around her feet, sand crabs labor sideways, their eyes moist, human, trapped looking. The beach ends abruptly, and she takes a path leading to the narrow road with its nickings of stone and glass, the pain a joy against her feet.

Walking now past lightless wooden shacks on tottering brick foundations, past the Gospel Hall Church, a block of yellow stucco with windows shaped like rowboats. The fish market a gutted darkness with fish-taint, heavy as tarp, persistent.

By daylight she has seen village men dragging sacks bloated and bumpy with fish up the beach from their boats, upending them, slips of mercury raveling over spread-out newspapers, flies moving in, sparkling. Squat, mesolithic-busted women in tight, mismatched outfits and baseball caps, yelling prices for yellow dolphin, flying fish, women with string bags and cardboard boxes on their heads, buying fish rolled in newspaper. Now the market is black, echoing, pungent.

* * *

So I tell you, man, this grieving white woman in a fancy white dress, she's going like some damn starve cat, prowling dirt paths, she trip over the garbage between shacks, this resort white stops then to hear this one baby cry, she listen, alert as anything, hungry like she want to take that baby between her fingers like some meat . . . us sitting on curbs like we do, outside the bars, she asks that we make obscenities to eat at her, she is that anyhow, she is telling us, salt eaten up. She has a dead child, she is telling us. Inside the bar she is asking you know, for rum. Then she thinks we climb like market flies on her. Get away. She flings her speech you know, packs her talk into what she calls our open monkey-faces. I have a baby child, a girl dead, she keeps forever telling.

So two of us, one at either elbow, we decide better to walk this poor damn white lady out of our town, so we take her back, cross her over to the whites' resort like she is some dangerous thing, some bomb . . .

* * *

In their hotel room, Renee stands on the straw mat. Only the bathroom light is on.

Bill? I heard a baby inside one of those terrible shacks the people live in. It kept crying and crying. The sound went right through me.

Grayish fluorescent light halos her body. Renee steps out of its glare, closer to the bed.

I was going up and down their streets, running, yelling, I think I was yelling, like a crazy person. God. Anyone could have done anything, hurt me, killed me. They must certainly, in some way, hate us. But those people, Bill? Those two men? They didn't listen, didn't do anything to me like I might have wanted.

What they did, those men, was take hold. Just take hold, as if I were some lost, precious child, and bring me back.

Ramon: Souvenirs

My wife met Ramon at the cold-frame nursery where she worked. It was late May, when some of the Pueblo farmers would come by to get extra green chili seedlings. Luana lifted and slid wooden flats into the blue truckbed while he angled around for his wallet. She was counting out change from the leather purse at her waist when he started telling her she was as pretty as the pink and white flowers blooming all behind her.

I get sporadic news from Luana, a few fuzzed snapshots of her kids. The letters come with me inside a squat adobe house which slumps like unfired clay next to the two-lane highway going north to Santa Fe, south to Albuquerque. Occasionally I see Ramon driving by in the blue pickup, a roll of pink chiffon around his dark forehead, his sister's children in the back. If he's alone, he'll sometimes stop. Then we sit on cottonwood stumps I rolled through the front door after Luana shipped her chairs to Chicago. We drink beer, we don't exactly converse. There are barriers of language, of my ex-wife, still thick between us.

In Berkeley, Luana'd started by thumbtacking a poster of Sitting Bull on the ceiling above our loft-bed and carrying home books about American Indian cultures. I hitchhiked with her to an Indian arts fair in San Francisco. Rows and rows of hard-faced sellers, none of them Indian, murmuring prices like a hissing of dry horsetail, jacked-up prices for waxed turquoise and silver jewelry. In back of one booth I lifted a chunk of green rough-cut turquoise out of a cardboard box. These people, I figured, had already ripped the Indians. I was happy ripping them, maybe they deserved it.

We rode a bus into the city one night to see a benefit film at the American Indian Shelter. On the landing, above steep unlit stairs, Indians stood in groups, the men wearing jeans and T-shirts, strips of carmine cloth wound into their braided hair, the women becalmed like neglected ships and barnacled with sober, wide-cheeked children. Luana, who had been reading about North American native cultures, was confused by these Indians who stood around ignoring her interest in them. Under the fluorescent lighting, our faces belonged to our ancestors, our guilt was undiluted by the arrival of any other visitors.

We sat in an unheated auditorium and saw a film about the destruction of Indian cultures, a sad and hopeless kind of film. At my insistence, we crept out before its conclusion, before the laboratory lighting pinned us like specimens to an empty mounting of tan metal chairs.

Luana kept on, transporting sacks of canned goods, donating odds and ends from our closets and cupboards to the Indian Shelter in Oakland, things like a National Geographic globe, a ceramic cow with a hole in its paislied snout for pouring cream.

Next she wanted to move to New Mexico, to find Indians preserved, unembittered, in the resin of reservations. The desert's low humidity would be good for my work; the Bay Area was in the midst of another earthquake panic. I could think of no objection.

So in January, Luana saw her reservation Indians crossing snow-blurred, unpaved roads, inclining drunkenly into a sunset false as a painted scrim. We were in Gallup, a haggard town overloaded with pawnshops, liquor stores, trading posts, and gray cinderblock bars. In the motel someone started hammering and cursing at our door; I opened it and a boy with whiskey slopped down his shirt took two giant steps and fell grinning, unconscious, across our bed. So we left, driving past a run-down Dairy Queen with a bead-string of children queued up. They stood with rooted patience, with an inertia I had never associated with children. Square orange papers, white napkins, wax cups rolled and caught around their thin legs, then blew like blighted pollen across the desert. We drove through Albuquerque, kept going north. In the Spanish town of Bernalillo we rented a pink stucco house with peeling linoleum floors and hospital green walls. I set up my workbench while Luana built a Navajo loom from pine, doweling, and rope. She sat on the hardpacked plot of fenced dirt that was our yard, washing and spinning raw wool, turning lumpy skeins in pails of dye made from onion skins, marigold heads, walnut shell. She made a saddle blanket, uneven and dusky, of which she was very proud.

By chance we found this dilapidated adobe house near the Rio Grande with its red clay floors, stuccoed hump of fireplace, and wooden vigas striping the white ceilings. We paid rent with the lutes I made, and Lu took a job at the cold-frame nursery down the road for forty dollars a week.

With her first paycheck, she bought an Indian cookbook, and we began eating things like posole, red chili stew, rabbit stew, fried squash blossoms, blue corn tortillas. She drove out to the Pueblo ceremonial dances, watching with an absorbed, mournful intensity. I sometimes went along, but cultural voyeurism makes me uneasy and it was dispiriting, the gritty white turf of tossed beer and whiskey bottles along the roadsides into the reservations, our being checked to make sure we had not brought in a camera or notebook.

Luana went to ceremonials as well as furtively stalking Indian families in discount stores, sitting in roadside cafés, straining to overhear their conversations. But until Ramon padded up in his gray, earth-stained trousers, his thinning hair knotted at the nape of his neck, and told her she was as pretty as the pink and white flowers that bloomed all behind her, she had not met or spoken to one Indian.

She invited him into our house. We shook hands. I held out a beer, noticing that several of his teeth were missing and the remainder looked fairly close to dissolution. I was amused, initially, at my wife's having lured home an Indian to examine at close range. Ramon was illiterate, his use of English confined to the practical. But he had mastered certain phrases which he flashed at Luana, dazzlingly bridging the cultural abyss between them. "You're pretty, I like you. Pretty girl. I like you." I know this because my workshop abuts the kitchen, so while I was planing down strips of curly maple, gluing and clamping struts across the pear-faces of lutes, the two of them kept busy as well, bandying their courtship across the kitchen table.

Luana quickly grew fat-witted over Ramon's attentions. She rode a bus into Albuquerque to gather up library recordings of Pueblo corn-grinding songs, rabbit-skinning songs, water-fetching songs, each accompanied by a cultural monograph. She put up her red hair in a butterfly bun, wore suede moccasins, velveteen blouses, long puffy skirts.

With humorless zeal, she wove on her loom, spelling herself back into some ancient world sieved from books, old photographs, exhibits, and her own cryptic needs. Whatever she knew or understood of him, Luana was convinced Ramon would be her ticket into a mythic, far better world. He would instead prove to be that single loose thread in a Navajo weaving, the lightning path, or spirit escaped.

While I saw him as a farmer, a cultivator of squash, chilies and pumpkin, one eye cocked to the weather, the other to a pretty girl, Luana insisted on seeing legends in his clove-black, rheumy eyes. And watching Lu anchor herself to this one old man, I gambled on tolerance as a selfless virtue for which I would, in time, be rewarded.

When Ramon mentioned he didn't have a traditional dance kilt, Luana did library research and began to warp and tortuously weave a six-by-three-and-a-half-foot white ceremonial garment. With no design or color to challenge her, she sat cross-legged on the red floor, throwing the shuttle with its knob of cotton string back and forth, slamming down the oak batten. When this piece, which would be overlaid with red, black, and green symbols, was cut down from the loom, Luana worried over its imperfections. She expected that such patient labor would earn her way into the secretive maze of Pueblo culture.

So it was an ironic moment when she held out the stiffly rolled bundle to Ramon and he looked eagerly and straight across it to her breasts. Their fantasies, it appeared, had diverged.

That summer he often stopped at the nursery or our house. One afternoon in July his pickup lurched into the driveway. Our five dogs leapt raggedly at the gate as three women and several children trailed Ramon into the yard.

Ramon's daughters and grandchildren bunched modestly in our living room. As Luana greeted them, I leaned against the doorway of my shop, waiting for these women to acknowledge me, look at me. They never did. One of them, Marie Therese, gave my wife a round hive-shaped bread. The other two stood near the door, smiling at whatever was said. After fifteen minutes of their hyperbolic smiling, Ramon herded the group out. Leaning in to close the front door, he shot a lewd wink at my wife.

That smooth hump of loaf, it turned out, was a fertility symbol. Whose baby? I wondered, tapping absently at the crust, brooding over the turn things were taking. When she returned from the yard, Lu was eager to explain the women's indifference to me. Pueblo culture was matriarchal; women carried the power of the bloodline. They stirred the pot, they owned the pot. When a husband found his belongings stacked outside a closed front door, he had been asked to leave. Imagine that, I said.

Weeks later, the fertility loaf untouched and taking up precious freezer space, Ramon came by to invite us to some kind of feast day at the Pueblo. One of the queerer things about this man and myself was how affably he cuckolded me and how agreeable I was to being cuckolded; yet it always seemed absurd, calling rival to a harmless old man. My wife was infatuated with the culture, not the man. It would pass. So we drank goodnaturedly together, I ate at his family's table, and Ramon was not without his wits. Inviting a married couple would be far more acceptable to his relatives than bringing young Luana alone. False scent, that was me.

Ramon drove us into the reservation, alongside rows of low adobe squares, clay dominoes with small dark dots of windows. Probably Luana anticipated black pottery brimming with rabbit stew, hollow gourds holding fermented maize. The feast her books and museum trips had led her to expect. The feast of one hundred years ago.

We followed him through a low doorway. In the center of a shadowy, low-ceilinged room with a dirt floor stood a picnic table covered with a flowered oilcloth over which was spread a bill-board jumble of cookies, soft drinks, potato chips, Twinkies, cakes with pink icings. There were no formal introductions, so, at something of a social loss, I sat on a bench alongside one wall. Ramon sat beside me, popped a can of beer, and eyed Luana, who sat at the picnic table beside a sullen-faced teenage boy. Ramon indicated this was his sister's place—he tilted his head in the direction of an elderly woman lifting a kettle onto a stove and wiping her hands on a blue dishcloth.

Lu tinkered around with a stalled conversation, her glib bright questions clunking like wrenches dropped on cement. In a confession to me much later that night, she admitted that the boy's silence, coupled with his overt gawking at her, had led her to assume, in a grand and foolish mental jeté, that he was mildly retarded. So she stayed beside him, her whole pose alert with new pity. Ramon and I, having run out of topics, drank our beers.

With an urgent, guttural noise, the boy pointed to a curtained doorway, then to Luana. With theatrical compassion, Luana interpreted slowly and loudly . . . "OH, YOU WANT ME," here she pointed at herself, "TO GO WITH YOU, OVER THERE . . ." She pointed to a doorway with an orange bedspread nailed across it.

He nodded, repeated his pantomime. With the poise of a social worker, she rose and followed the boy behind the curtain.

Ramon stared, the good nature knocked off his face. I was onto my third or fourth beer, but not unaware that Ramon's sister had stiffened and turned away, the hospitality blown out of her too. A subdued Marie Therese stood drying this one plate over and over; then she got busy flapping curious children outside with her towel.

In trying to escape, Luana got caught in the tasseled fringe of the bedspread. As she was struggling, the boy sidled out from the other side, pulling up the zipper of his jeans and with a thwarted but voluptuous expression buckling his belt. He left the house, banging the screen door.

Ramon sat like a victim. Luana practically belly-crawled across the room to Marie Therese, who understood the most English.

"I swear, I thought he wanted to show me something in his room. A rock collection or something. I'm sorry. I didn't understand at all. We didn't do anything. Oh God. I didn't understand what he was talking about *at all*."

Marie Therese said something like that's ok, he's always acting like that, he's just a bad boy. Then she went straight to her old aunt and rattled off the story. The silver-haired aunt turned to Luana, grinning, and Luana closed her eyes briefly, grateful for being forgiven. Ramon, comprehending that he had not lost her to one of his insolent nephews, pulled himself up, grinning, as if at some joke.

That incident behind us, we sat down to eat hot red chili, wiping our bowls with chunks of fry bread.

Later, when Lu helped Mary Agnes clear off the table, Ramon limped outside to start up his truck. I propped myself against the wall, watching him gun the engine, while this same nephew emerged out of the summer blackness, pressing a joint into my hand.

He nodded to Ramon's tortoise-like profile through the dusty truck window. "Don't let Pops catch on, he's not too cool." Returning his peace sign, I noted how subtly, like smoke, he was breathed back into the dark clay corridors of the Pueblo.

On the drive home from the reservation I stuck my head out of the truck window, numbed by the desert wind, the soporific wind, preferring not to see Ramon's hand slipping into the soft yawn of Luana's thighs, but seeing it in detail, knowing it would all happen anyway.

At an overpriced Mexican restaurant, over too much red wine, Luana unearthed, moved in different patterns, assigned various weights to her paltry excavations. "He's asked for a picture of my mother. He says if he could be any wild animal, he'd be a wild turkey. His wives, he's had two, both died after long sicknesses. He has dogs that sleep on his bed with him. He's been in the Bernalillo jail twice for drunk driving and was in a crash up in the Sandias . . . his father wouldn't allow him to go to school because he had to tend the goats, and now he can't read or write. Imagine passing by billboards and not having to read them. His church, he told me, is in the center of his forehead between his eyes, that's just like the Hindus, isn't it?"

Then, dropping a more precious vessel than the rest, she blurted out, "Ramon's impotent, you know. So once in a while I just let him touch me. He's lonely so I decided I really don't mind."

Angel of compassion. I'd always liked that about Luana.

"It's his diabetes. One of the side effects, but I have to tell you, it's so amazing. Really. He has this totally different way of touching than American men. He makes you feel fertile, earthy. Like sex isn't sex but some worship of the earth mother in you. A spiritual lust for the female body . . ."

I scraped the bittersweet mole sauce off my food while reminding Lu that I disliked this type of restaurant, expending its effort on decor and funking out on the damned food. I preferred an unpretentious café, spotted oilcloth, cracked dishes.

When we got home, I unlatched the back gate, the dogs flowing past, speckled, spawning, onto the sandy ditchbank. We walked out past the horse corral, orchards, grass fields loaded with quail and pheasant, cottonwoods with black and white guinea fowl pegged to the branches. The dogs lolloped in scattered directions, tails stiff-up, noses rooting, dirt-rimmed. I was finally weary of the entire Ramon misadventure, out of patience and sick of it. And I knew Luana was thinking of nothing else.

On the small planked bridge, a miserly cut of moon above us, we sat watching a muskrat shudder and bump against the weedy ditchbank.

"I want to go live with him. If I can. I need to be with him."

I might have argued with her or slapped her possessed face. Claimed her somehow. Instead, my nature upheld this persistent conviction that to love was to let go and to be in fairly constant pain over it.

Ramon now felt free to walk into our house without knocking. One particular time proved to be the crucial test of Luana's infatuation. Ramon came in wearing a blue chiffon scarf, turquoise bolo tie and western plaid shirt, and I don't know what they said to one another, I was at the band saw tearing up strips of maple for the back of a new lute and couldn't hear. But after a while Lu and I were in the Volkswagen, tailing Ramon up to the reservation. A few miles outside Santo Domingo the truck bounced off the road in front of a gray cinderblock bar with a neon sign swaying off one edge. Ramon's face, his tumid eyes, pressed fishlike against our window. Smiling. "We stop for a beer."

Eerie as a weekday in church, that bar. No music, no air conditioning, no TV, no tables or chairs. Nothing. A small fan revolved behind the bar, aimed at the bartender. Just Indians, no sociability about it, drinking. One had slid down a wall, passed out, numbed. Ramon answered the bartender's greeting and ordered three beers. The younger men had long, loose hair, wore T-shirts and jeans; there were a few like Ramon with their rolled chiffon headbands, silvering hairknots, and bolo ties. The place was dark, airless, a cell. Fly-dotted amber strips spiraled from the low ceiling, green squares of linoleum were worn through to dirt. There was a mess in the urinal, so I went out back, pissed into dry red earth, cracked into pieces like an imageless puzzle.

They were strangely incurious toward Luana and me, sitting white and foreign up at the bar. Ramon set his emptied bottle back on the counter, and I paid for the three of us.

Back in our car, we stuck close behind Ramon's truck. On long curves, when his truck wobbled off into the juniper scrub, we'd wait until it nudged like some nosing reptile onto the highway again.

We entered the reservation, but instead of taking the road into the Pueblo, Ramon turned onto a second, higher road, and after several miles of nothing but overbright scoured hills and scrub piñon we passed a corroded windmill, a boarded-up trading post, general store, and gas station, its windows smashed, its pumps propped like red obelisks in front.

Dirt and rocks slewed up as we bumped along the unpaved road, at the end of which stood a federal project house, uncolored, bleak as the utilitarian mind that had conceived it, corralled by a wallow of animal pens, sagging barb fences, and a muddy, urine-watered farmyard.

Ramon parked close to the open porch, its warped surface a green-white moonscape of chicken shit. The front door sloped open as if it had lost any sense of function. Ramon stood hospitably beside its torn screen, saying, "Come in, come in." As I got out of the car a big, wide-shouldered Indian over by a wooden shed turned and glared at us, then turned away. He was hammering out what looked like silver jewelry, on a tree stump.

The house stank of animal. We followed Ramon down a hall into the kitchen, glare-washed, its objects lost in an aura of obtrusive west sunlight. Chickens panicked, flapped off chairs, squawked down the hall to the porch where one peered back in with a jelly-dark, insulted eye. A baggy black dog with a matt of burrs on one ear lay listless or feigning death in a corner of the kitchen. Ramon wanted to pour us coffee, but Luana blanched as she looked down at the stove, its original porcelain finish buried

beneath a blackened mask of boiled-over meals. From one of the
back rooms, Creedence Clearwater Revival collided with the rural
silence pouring in from open windows

   . . . rollin'   rollin'   rollin' on the river . . .

A bony child of about fourteen with waist-length hair and
wearing only jeans glided barefoot into the kitchen. Introduced
himself as Peter, opened the refrigerator, took out a can of soda,
and drank. Looked at us with friendly amusement. Ramon sat at
the table, ill at ease.

I wondered, did he dress and eat and sleep to the background
of rock music played by his sons? That would be reason enough
for his aimless driving up and down the highways, stopping off in
bars, even seeking refuge in our house, where native songs borrowed from the library, the old songs, scratched on in some familiar way.

We both refused coffee again, and Peter had gone back to his
room, so Ramon ushered us back outside to the animal pens.
Goats jammed against one another, shoving up to the fence, rearing on hind legs so we could scratch their bristled, knobby heads.
Quite empty, their eyes, the rectangular pupils like black strips of
negative across the grass-yellow iris, the ribs like barrel staves jutting from thin sides.

The Indian I had first seen, the big-shouldered one, was walking toward us. A silver medallion swung on his naked chest. Peter
had said this was his older brother, Nick. Walking toward us, a
hostile scowl on his face, then abruptly he veered off toward the
house, banged up onto the porch, kicked the door back viciously,
and went inside.

We said good-bye to Ramon, it seemed time to do that, and
backed the Volkswagen down the rutted lane, leaving him bent
over a sack of grain, spraying out feed in an almost gentle obei-
sance to his animals.

Luana was quiet on the ride home, her head turned out the
window, but when I mentioned that there were a lot of dead ani-

mals, both wild and domestic, on these back roads, animals who had gotten unwary from so little traffic and were now so much accidental waste, she turned to me, as I remember, eyes steeped in some other meaning, and agreed.

Late that August, Ramon came by to invite us to the Corn Dance. Luana had not been saying much about Indians or Ramon since our visit. She walked each morning to the nursery to water and sell stunted, imported flowers demanded by the easterners who had retired to the desert for reasons of health, and found themselves innately repelled by it. Afternoons when there were no customers she sat under slatted shade on metal bins of grass seed, reading tree and shrub catalogues. I was repairing a seventeenth-century harp for a local historian. My reputation as a craftsman was gaining, I was finding a good place for myself. Luana's purpose seemed increasingly uncertain and strained. We had grown scrupulously kind to one another, though there was a deadness at the core of our fine manners.

The day of the Corn Dance we rode in the back of a neighbor's pickup, part of a long string of vehicles headed for the Pueblo. Hitchhikers jumped in until the truckbed sagged. Someone passed a joint, a bottle of red wine went around. Lu kept apart, sitting with her hands strapped around her knees, staring at what were now for her disappointing, barren mountains.

An Indian in a Texas hat and reflector sunglasses signaled us to a parking spot. He gave us mimeoed programs: WELCOME TO THE SANTO DOMINGO CORN DANCE. PLEASE. NO DRINKING. NO CAMERAS. THANK YOU.

There had been no rain in over a month. The sky, no different from yesterday's, was pulled taut from one dry rim to another.

As tourists, we were compressed into a tight arc around the dancers in the central plaza. Out of habit I pointed out Ramon among the chorus of old men. Luana nodded but didn't look in that direction.

The male dancers wore white kilts, their naked chests streaked with clay, their high moccasins lifting and falling upon earth worn slightly concave by ancestors praying for distant-fallen rains. The women danced barefoot, wearing black dresses and wooden head-dresses. All of the people waved branches of evergreen; the drum-beat was unvaried, unceasing, timed to the human heart. I developed a headache from the noon sun and the drum's pulse. Luana's face was blistered with sweat. The old men in their brilliant shirts and loose white trousers, silver hair bound up, raised thin feet in a ghostly motion, chanting. Among them, Ramon looked surprisingly stolid, earthly.

What was his place among these people? Why did he live alone in a government house outside the community? As I watched him, I thought he lacked the religious intensity of the old men surrounding him. He looked hot, several times bringing out a handkerchief to wipe his brow.

The dance would go on for hours. Until it rained. In the late afternoon a single cloud, black, false-looking, moved as if towed over the square plaza, over the people's crow-black, gleaming heads. Rain freckled the dust around their lifting feet, mixed in a sweaty glaze down their backs and chests and faces. And behind the shadowed privacy of her dark glasses, Luana was crying, watching them shimmer in black and white lines before her, out of reach.

Luana gave up the music and the weaving, and discarded us both. She moved out of the house and by summer's end had gone to the Northwest and enrolled in graduate school. She married, moved to Illinois, where the only reminder of Indians might be in the street signs, scout troop names, names of recreational lakes and campgrounds. Her last letter said the two children were fine, that she was organizing a peace awareness program in their school. She had converted to her husband's faith, Roman Catholicism. Surprisingly, she asked about my work, my music, even suggesting that I let her know if I needed financial help. Not once has she asked about Ramon or referred to the Indian people who so obsessed her that summer.

When Ramon stopped by, I had to tell him Luana had left us. I took advantage, giving him the rest of her things. A picture of her out by the horse corral, her hair in long braids. A saddle blanket she'd made, more pictures. I wanted the house shaken clean, emptied of her. He accepted everything, as seemingly passive at her loss as I had been. The loom I gave away at a flea market. With an anger I had never allowed while she lived there, I ravaged the house.

The following summer my father became ill. In the fall he died of cancer. I had flown to Los Angeles and stayed until after the funeral. The day I returned home I sat out on the front step, turning the pages of Dad's Bible. He'd made these notes everywhere, underlining passages, putting rows of exclamation points beside them. Reminded me of Luana, in a funny way. The enthusiasm.

Ramon's truck hauled into the driveway, sat like some hunk of polished plastic turquoise. A thin blonde girl trailed him into the yard, then knelt to pet the dogs. She was not as pretty as Luana. Ramon and I shook hands, the girl jumped up and introduced herself. I'd already guessed what she did, where she worked, but I asked.

"I work down the road, you know, the cold-frame nursery? That's where we met . . ." She looked at him with those exact same eyes. Proud. Overbright.

I recalled his son Peter's amusement, his other son's contempt, the implication that Luana had not been the first. I came up with a laugh, surprising myself. Ramon laughed as well, and as if in conspiracy with me, clamped an arm around my shoulders. Later, as we walked back to the truck, the girl tagging behind, he complained of numbness in his feet and pointed to a cataract growing like blue-white lichen over his left eye. His health wasn't so good, he said.

Ramon backed his truck onto the highway, pointed north towards the reservation. He waved, the girl smiled and waved, then Ramon turned, his shrunken profile set behind the rigid wheel of machinery. The young girl, caught by her own dreamings, stared straight ahead.

With Wings Cross Water

Overlarge, matte crow of death pegged to the underside, the staved-in ark of me. Blue-black reaper in conjured shape of a gloomy bird. Mute, it has performed nothing. Up to now. Why shouldn't any of us, if chance favors, turn our backs on its blunt, vigilant spectacle?

* * *

The coarse girth of the crow swells in Mrs. Grant, flooding the interior of the car so that when the navy-blue station wagon turns onto the gravel road marked Watervale Inn, pressed against the car windows are weighty spatulate feathers, an incurious eyesphere, turning this way, then that.

It is noon.

"The Grants are here!" someone shouts from the tennis courts. Everyone looks. A few wave. Someone wearing a white visor lifts an arm to serve the ball.

* * *

Mr. Grant pulls at the screen door, ducks his head before stepping in.

"Whoops. Looks like they haven't got around to cleaning up for us yet."

Mrs. Grant, facing the first of Watervale's perennial disruptions, is annoyed. Undisturbed, Mr. Grant docks their suitcases on a bed awash with pitched sheets, pillows, and blankets from previous vacationers. The Grants' six-year-old daughter demands the whereabouts of her bathing suit; the baby whines, wanting hers too, both children peevish from the numbing confinement of the car. The lake, just across the gravel road, down a slight grassy embankment, is in plain unbearable sight. Mr. Grant unloads the car while the girls run about touching everything, opening the small refrigerator, flushing the toilet, turning on the faucets. In their midst, Mrs. Grant thinks: unpack, sort the children's clothing into drawers and closets, keep a keen eye on them this week. That the lake is so near to their door frightens her. Her responsibilities have not lessened, only shifted location.

"Maybe you should take the children down to the lake while I straighten up here?"

A simple plan which includes trenching about for suits and beach towels, unzipping, tying straps, changing a soiled diaper, biting out a knot in the strings of the baby's bonnet. Plus the children, white as veal, demand all manner of props to protect them from the afternoon sun.

Finally they have gone. The screen door whimpers, falls shut.

Mrs. Grant does not unpack or organize. She goes into the tiny damp bathroom, shuts the door, undoes her blouse. Her fingers, working the left breast just above the nipple, quail and stop at the hard shores of it, her eyes focusing beyond red and blue candle stubs on the white shelf of the toilet, beyond gold curtains sucked in and out of the window by a breeze off the lake. The unfairness of what she feels, the unnerving persistence of it, makes Mrs. Grant feel weak, wishing she could cry out or faint. She fastens her blouse and goes out of the bathroom to sweep sand over the hump of doorsill, drag open stuck drawers, and fold away her family's clothes, thinking these clothes will be hurled to the four corners in a half-day's time, the stocked drawers emptied.

She hears them. The splash of water. Voices. So happy. The family. Without her.

* * *

The three-story Inn, which fronts Herring Lake, has been newly painted, a grayish green tint of common lichen. Spaced evenly above the white railed porch are mossy baskets of pink and red impatiens, and placed along the length of the porch are black iron chairs, glass-topped tables. Next to the screen door hangs the bulletin board with announcements, lost and found notices, sign-ups for tournaments and activities. Each year Mr. Grant signs up for nearly everything. The first year, Mrs. Grant appeared briefly in the tennis tournament; if she glances at the board anymore, it is only to find where her husband will be that day.

Mr. Grant shoulders the baby, catches his other daughter by the hand, and walks through the lobby with its yolk-yellow wicker, floral carpet, walls spotted with regional, priced artwork, goes into the main dining room. Mrs. Grant has unpacked the baby's bottle and bib, is setting up the high chair. The twelve or fifteen tables are dressed out with white cloths; in their centers stand green bottles stuffed with wild sweet pea and creamy Queen Anne's lace. Kitchen doors flail back and forth as college girls in white uniforms carry trays of food. Black fan blades blur on the cracked beige ceiling. The dining room is crowded and noisy with families; the baby yowls indignantly as Mrs. Grant, flushed from a potent cocktail, a dusty handprint on her cheek, straps her into the plastic chair. Buttering a square of homemade bread, Mr. Grant wonders how his wife can manage to look so lovely even while harassed. He is thinking of a way to compliment her on this when she stares over at him.

"Would you please help me with the baby? She's being impossible and I've had it."

He walks the baby back and forth on the porch until he is told that dinner is served.

After dessert, the guests' children run to feed their dinner crackers to clouds of khaki-colored fish drifting in shallow water beneath the pier. Toddlers dribble crumbs with stiffened arms, older children drop to their bellies, trying to scoop out fish prodding the surface for soggy flecks of cracker. The guests sit on the porch with their coffee or stand on the patio above the pier, watching.

The children are absolutely safe here. Everyone watches. That is what Mr. Grant thinks. Mrs. Grant thinks her children could both drown in full sight of everyone. Just because people are there doesn't mean they see.

* * *

An hour or so before dark, the families walk down to the Big Beach. Hike up the steep dune past the crawl of grapevine, the clumps of white leaning birch. Shadows rise up the dune, spilling down in long gray lengths to the edges of Lake Michigan. Plaid blankets are laid down, canvas beach chairs unfolded, children circle and spin like blown seeds down the dunes, babies burrow toes and fingers into the bluish sand, sit up, ears and mouths comically dribbling with its cold grit. The sun prepares to cast itself reliably into the lake, performing nightly for these guests, assembled like bright, well-fed gulls.

The dark red sun balances, slips into its slot of lake. There is a smattering of applause, the call for an encore. Firewood is searched out, heaped up, matches are struck. The children gather into the heat, their gilded faces rapt as angels', roasting marshmallows on peeled sticks.

Mrs. Grant carries the baby up toward the bonfire, having retrieved her from the booming edge of the lake where she was occupied with washing rocks. Mr. Grant, talking with an old friend, smiles, happily complacent, at the sight of his wife laboring up the dune, her jeans rolled above her freckled calves, her sweatshirt pulled off one shoulder by the baby's fist. Their older daughter runs down to push a bit of charred marshmallow into her mother's laughing, wrenched mouth. The baby grabs at the sticky goo and rubs it into her curly hair, pokes her sticky fingers into her mother's ear.

The Grants, understandably, are tired from their long drive. Friends wish them good night as they gather their things to walk back down the dune, follow the dirt road back to the guest cottages and the Inn. The baby bobbles sleepily along in her stroller; three pairs of sandals and a sweatshirt are hooked onto its red plastic handles. Their other daughter says she smells skunk and complains, while yawning, that she isn't tired yet. She asks what stars are made of. Why are they drawn with points if they don't have points? It is so uniquely peaceful, this summer's night, that the Grants pass their room and walk onto the pier, out to its edge, look at the night sky, the black glitter of the lake, the high full forms of trees. Water rocks the planks like a cradle; the windows of the Inn glow behind them.

As she hears her husband tell their daughter about the flaming balls of gases that are stars, inhospitable to life and one thousand or more times larger than the sun, Mrs. Grant thinks how the universe has become a consistently colder place as she has aged. She gazes into the lake, imagines the army of green fish swarming there; she is afraid of dark water, the rushing of impersonal slips of life crowding beneath its surface. So she looks away from the disturbing inhabitants of water and up to the stars, to flaming uncontrollable mixtures. Without points. The nursery world dismantled, stick by stick. Was she so guilty, singing pretty rhymes to her babies in the dim-lit powdery nursery, Wynken, Blynken and Nod, God will watch, never fear, cows jumping over the moon, cats with their fiddles aloft . . . did she sing to comfort herself, to believe in things that the world never intended to have?

Her mother died of breast cancer. A damning fact which makes Mrs. Grant's feet and hands turn icy-heavy. She rolls the stroller back and forth on the pier in a panicky, caught rhythm.

The children are asleep in their sandy beds. In the bare vacation room, light bulbs glaring, Mr. Grant slides his hands around his wife's waist. Mrs. Grant is exhausted from the long day. Nothing to give, she says. Apologizes. So Mr. Grant lies behind her in bed, rubbing the spot between her shoulder blades where she always likes. He has fallen asleep, she knows he has left her when his hand slows, stops, falls heavily off her back as if, well, dead.

Late into that night and the next, Mrs. Grant's eyes are dry and staring. She listens for her own private gloss of blood, for some new interference in its slick curving course, hears it in the siege and shake of dour black wings.

* * *

Mrs. Grant's powers of observation inflate. Out of her doomed, provisionally mortal body, she can see with the hyperacuity of an artist, or saint, an angel of Rilke's, perhaps. On an early morning walk she sees the white raft floating beyond the pier as a severe white cube, eerily placed between a sky and lake so equally blue, brumous, soft that there is no line of demarcation, only this cube, white, disembodied, pure as math. When she leaves the Inn after breakfast, the lake has wrested itself from the sky, asserted its greenish daylight surface. Gulls with black heads and wings plod like chess pawns across the solid raft. The world has regained mass, density, its imperfection.

But every such vision of Mrs. Grant's has its darkly poised counterpart. Before she is fully awake, her hand is on the laconic stubborn weight fixed inside her soft breast. Her own body lies superimposed like tabbed paperdoll clothes upon the stiff, drugged form of her mother in those final hospital days. And finally, Mrs. Grant summons up no further vision at all. Even black too simple for what she has to face.

* * *

On vacation Mr. Grant likes to play tennis and golf. Mrs. Grant, who normally seeks shade, privacy, and intelligent literature, does not want to be alone. She wants her children, sits uncharacteristically on noon-hot beaches with them, stands hatless and hip deep in the greenish skim of lake, swinging the baby in yellow, frothing circles until her arms ache, talking in that disconnected way familiar to mothers of small, interrupting children. Fish press their mouths against her gleaming calves. She is as impressed by her children's importunities as by their casual and stunning displays of affection for her; wonders if it is in the broad and egocentric nature of all children to both neglect and overwhelm. Even her husband's reliance on her whole and healthy capabilities is no less real than the children's. She suddenly knows that he will be, when she is taken from the body of their family, most broken, most easily lost.

Mrs. Grant is collecting the Snoopy raft, the McDonald's beach buckets, damp sandy towels, hoisting up her clammy-suited baby, accepting a friend's offer to watch her other daughter, when she feels its black wings engulf her, tenderly enough. She feeds the baby, changes the diaper, puts her in her crib, closes the door. Fumbles for her thin, burnt-orange copy of *The Duino Elegies,* and sits on the cement apron outside their rooms, sits with Rilke's book on a webbed lawn chair. Holds the book and doesn't read.

On the porch railing above her head, beach towels hang like crumpled cartoons. A baseball game, static flaring and fading, has been left on someone's radio. A car rolls by as if melting, dust heaving from under its tired black wheels. Mrs. Grant cannot see who is inside. She thinks about the year before, when there was a migration of dying monarch butterflies. Butterflies by the thousands, weak, dying, carpeting the beaches with black and orange mosaic, a lifting and frail falling of wings. No one could explain why. The horrifying abundance in nature. The casual waste. Maybe the silver canoes scattered around the lake's rim like dark split seedpods had reminded her. Mrs. Grant can suddenly stand no more of summer.

Clutches her book, opens the screen door by its definite black knob (round dull lusterless crow eye is an old black doorknob, isn't it?), lies face upward on the colorless bedspread. Her imaginings desperate, acute, her head turns, mind inventories, to push off the hard black breasting of her fear . . .

Room with walls of watery beige, Turkish carpets sluffed away to white strings, riddled with sand and dropped like playing cards against the green floor. A wicker table beside my bed, on it a lamp, its base a bluehipped Almaden bottle. The picture window with blinds that dip, sag, on either side the indefinite color curtains with orange and brown splotches like bad rash plaguing them. They do not even close over the blinds, those ugly curtains. Everything sun-faded, sun-defeated, except the black nicked-up dresser with oval pulls. Overhead, a scalloped lamp held by fake brass chain. Summer debris strewn about, damp, balled-up clothing, paperbacks with crackle-glazed spines, tennis rackets, golf bag, soda cans, radio, cassette tapes, towels, sandals, coins, dead wildflowers, toys, and the tiny bathroom swamped with stuff, all moist-smelling. Through it to the children's darkened room, brown curtains with rocking horses on them, a back door opening to the scrubby little place with laundry lines. Baby sleeping in a sandy crib.

She finishes the rooms, lies there, lies as if already dead, yet her head heavily pivots, sees the healthy trees, good sky, sand, lake, mosquito-filamented air, hears the baseball game, feels it on the other side of the door, the screen door, August, the ordinary foolish assumptions of health and well-being from which she is now excluded. Mrs. Grant, hands crushed between her knees, knees inflexed to chin, begins to rock. Obtund repetition of grief.

* * *

After dinner a baby-sitter takes the two children down to the Big Beach for the sunset. The Grants go around to the backside of the Inn where gallon jars of tea steep in dry grass beneath clotheslines pinned and jowled with guests' white bedsheets. They walk past empty tennis courts, cross the two-lane road. There is an odd patch of woods to comment on, replanted by a lumber company some years before, where skinny-trunked pines jut out from the dirt like perfectly even rows of straight pins in a paper envelope.

They take the trail into the natural forest of pine, maple, fir, and birch. Walking with the preoccupation and pace of city people. They cannot talk; mosquitoes as well as tufts of white gnats surround them like a holy nimbus. On the dark, spongy floor are wild columbine, strawberry, fern, fungus, and snakeroot with its protuberant white eyes on red stems. The trail opens into a clearing of iron-red sumac, dry grasses, then turns into a second forest with surfs of waist-high evergreens to wade through, evergreens studded with scarlet berries like waxy candies. They climb over caved-in trunks of fallen trees, fungus frilling the rot. Insects shake, vibrate the air; in places it ripples like vapor. They grab onto tough-stemmed shrubs, scale a vertical hill of sand, climb up and out of beachlike valleys until they reach the mountain, a mountain of sand which drops off in an impressive vertical to Lake Michigan. The insects have kept in the dark forest, excepting a few dun grasshoppers with concealed wingspreads of poppy red. The Grants have their arms around one another's waists, looking down at the thin hem of rocky beach, the lake all mottled green and turquoise. The sun, a biblical, false red, is balanced in the evening sky. Mr. and Mrs. Grant have taken off their sweat-darkened clothing, the wind blows over their pale, exposed flesh.

Mr. Grant knows his wife's belly is softened, marked by the births of their daughters, her dropped breasts have tendrils of white scarring them. Nonetheless, or perhaps even more so, she remains beautiful. Mr. Grant feels himself hugely fortunate. He has been given what was promised. Asks his wife to join him on their clothing, spread out into a kind of blanket. Kissing her, he thinks to ask what it was she wanted, earlier, to tell him. Kissing her as she takes his hand over to one of her breasts. Insistently. Not erotically. Until he knows.

In crisis, he strives for optimism. He will have them both be-

lieve in the positive forces of science. The breakthroughs in medicine, the combinations of drugs. The role of attitude in control-
ling disease. In comparison, her mother's cancer was a long time
ago. And if it is cancer, her youth is a distinct advantage. Maybe it
isn't cancer. They are both so young for this.

Sit silent a while. She wipes her teary face with her husband's
plaid shirt, considers, then indulgently rubs her nose along the
shirt, making them both laugh.

He rolls up their clothes into two bundles. Readies them for
the race. Sets a mark. Shouts. They are off, sinking down and
springing up, diving in and whooping out of the deep, giving
sand, imploding, exploding, gleeful, hilarious, mad.

Then Mr. Grant trips. Grounded, rubbing his ankle, winded.
Sees his wife's arms striking like balsa blades, her legs chopping
feathers of sand. She descends the mountain, smaller and smaller
until he sees her turn, salute up to him, then plunge like an isolate
wreck, unprotected, into the dark curtain of water.

Mr. Grant feels it then. Feels it clamp down, permanent in the
perch of his rib, the dull-knobbed eye of it, the rustle, all gleam-
less, of common feather.

The glittering speck of her surfaces shouts to him.

Are you all right?

Standing gingerly, he waves and tries to run, defiant of that
which pains and assails him, down to his wife.

Shed of Grace

Graceless things, I told myself, are never loved.

A household fly lands upon threadlike legs which end in splayed, cabriole feet. No head to speak of, its oxblood eyes split by a puny spray of antennae. Even in patterns of flight, the fly remains graceless, a creature of annoyance.

I take sharp pleasure in slamming him into the desk top, in sweeping the dead pulp onto an envelope and removing it to the garbage. I should remember to ask Penelope's husband, when he returns here, if he finds any charm in burying the dead, in tamping down their final bit of property with one of his several shovels.

My impulsive sister Penelope has witlessly married a gravedigger and moved to this frayed town near a man-made lake, a lake encircled by deteriorating summer resorts and dispirited families. Penelope used to work as a model for photographed greeting cards. Whenever I visited the gift shop near my apartment, I would search among the rows of cards. I might find Penelope in a rowboat, holding a lace parasol over her egg-shaped blonde head, moving across a misted lake. She might be sitting on the pier, her slender legs like softening stems in a vase of clouded water. I sometimes discovered her running down steep grassy slopes, holding out a fistful of wildflowers, her hair in a thick, sun-riddled braid. An office acquaintance of mine bought one of these cards, the rowboat one I believe, and I commented on what a maudlin card it was. Offended, he claimed it was for his grandfather who was in a nursing home and was cheered by pretty things.

Pretty things. On the second day of my visit Penelope stood in the creek, cold water shackled to her calves, her hair a brilliant hinge between her shoulders. Unselfconsciously she waded, even with her puffed-out belly, so much like a bloated fish, purple stretch marks climbing up from her pubic area like winter vines. I watched as one watches any perfect creature, with furtive absorption, which bore on its underside murmurs of self-reproach.

From the moment I arrived I was asked to run errands and to perform favors. Only three days after I arrived I was asked to carry a black lunch pail to the cemetery. I chose to walk the mile and a quarter distance as it was not much more than I was accustomed to. I remember turning back the screen door as if it were a worn, oversoft book page and going down the grassy path of the sidewalk, the lunch pail a black speck in the corner of my eye, a black weight, anvil-like, in my hand.

These earliest days of October have sapped the foliage, leaving it brittle, yet along the road in front of Penelope's house stood several clumps of mauve-blooming phlox, ashen fungus furring the leaves, still pillaged by heavy-bodied insects. I passed beyond the shallow town, the single street with its church-owned thrift shop, boating shop, small grocery and drugstore; I passed the gas station and the bar, finally climbed the graveled incline. I should, after going down a short unpaved road, discover the cemetery.

Like most graveyards on the outskirts of blighted towns, its broad seclusion gave evidence that the majority of townspeople had taken final hospice here. I derive comfort from these modest gravesites, where a region's history is pared to brief, pale chronicles, where names are inflated to poetry by the absence of their fleshly owners. In the older section, with its filigreed enclosures of black ironwork so popular in the beginning of this century, leans one tongue-shaped stone, worn to white pumice, saying only BABY BOY, 1902. Most of these graves are overfanciful as if ornament lent balance to stark grief. Religious texts flow across stone in blurred teary script.

I became intrigued by a white shed, partially concealed by a clot of oak trees, some yards north of the creek dividing the cemetery (the same creek Penelope waded in). A wooden bridge with several badly charred posts spanned the narrow watercourse; I learned that on the other side were buried the original German settlers of this region. I did not cross the bridge, but went in some curiosity towards the shed. The door was unlatched, and I remember how tentatively I pushed it open.

The light resembled mottled tortoiseshell; the air smelled of stale earth. Dirt-caked shovels and spades of varying sizes were propped along one wall. Two wheelbarrows, one an old wooden one with a flat iron wheel, the other of green metal, leaned against the opposite wall. A plain oak desk was set beneath a window; on its surface was a large black book with a maroon label. Beside the book was a beer bottle, opened, emptied. A portable radio had been placed on the windowsill. Coils of dark hose, serpentine, took up one corner. Insects lay upturned along ledges or dried in sloppy webs in the corners of unwashed windows. I put the lunch pail on the desk and set my hand to the black book. But he pushed open the door then and I turned, seeing him in the sun-worked doorway, seeing the cloth tied around his forehead, the overalls, the muddied workboots. We greeted one another plainly enough, then went outside and sat together on the grass next to a hideous pink tombstone. A faded flag, jabbed into the ground beside it, stirred anemically. Nearby was a faucet; a green painted coffee can hung beneath the spigot. Water formed shape and fell into the bucket; a black lettered sign warned that the water was not fit to drink.

The mosquitoes had become fat and stupid as flies. He slapped at them without conscience as they landed on his skin, reminding me of the hide of an animal, cow or horse perhaps, when it shudders, involuntarily. One alighted on my forearm. I watched its transparent abdomen fill, turn plum-colored, then pressed my palm over its machinery and lifted up to expose the blotch of red polish, the body like discarded rind. Yellow jackets hovered near the gravedigger, drawn by the partially unwrapped food in the black lunch pail. I remember asking if they often stung him while he worked.

"Nothing bothers me," he said, taking great bites of food without offering to share any of it. When he was done, he lay back in the grass, arms crossed behind his head, eyes closed. I stared at him, at his body, all speech shrinking into a compressed silence inside me. Later he roused himself and, leaning on one elbow, studied me. I sat rigid, arms locked about my knees.

"Penelope tells me you've never had a boyfriend."

Resentful of his implications, I nearly told him that I compare my life to my sister's with pride, for it is a good deal more decent than hers. But I did not have the nerve or the skill to say this aloud.

He laughed, ignorant laughter, summoning up a childhood spent within close range of Penelope. I had long ago determined, as in a cautionary fable, that I should emerge morally superior, chastely triumphant, and untouched. This pride in my physical virtue had been my ballast in the world, enhanced by the distance I deliberately kept from her. Now, in this cemetery, an intimacy was formed in spite of Penelope, or because of her . . . as if his mouth forced breath into mine, and sound rushed from my lungs, in half-formed obscenities.

I have to rest now. Outside the rainwashed window of this shed I can watch the dark area spreading like a soaked tarp where I have begun to dig. The shovel stands upright in the ground, a leafless tree. The first time I went to the church in my neighborhood, hoping to have my own uprightness acknowledged in me, I waited outside the church afterward, to meet the priest who, like Penelope's husband, was younger than me and unpleasantly handsome. I stepped up to him and he took my hand, looked into my face and recognized nothing. Then his hand gave up its firmness, he looked to the person behind me, and I walked back in the noon sunlight to my apartment.

I left him pulling dead flowers out of vases. On the road back to my sister's house I had made up my mind that I should leave. I had begun to feel unwelcome and to fear that their worldly opinions of me would undo me, might unfasten the self I had prudently, independently constructed.

I helped Penelope to sew a quilt for the baby. As we sorted the soft squares of printed calico, she admitted that she wanted to model for greeting cards soon after the baby was born. She missed the money, and I knew, without her telling me, that this town where she was looked upon as a bit of lightning in a dense thicket had begun to oppress her in its complacent slide toward ruin. I also thought I detected in Penelope an impatience with her gravedigger husband. Perhaps like that of the townspeople's, his admiration hammered at her, in monotonous rhythm, lacking cleverness. Besides, Penelope preferred being slipped onto glass shelves in card shops, her image displayed and cheaply bought.

I have returned to my work; the hole is no deeper than when I left it to rest. Black clay sticks to the shovel and time and again I must scrape it off with my hands, which are crosshatched, raw, from grit hidden in the soil. Sin has great strength, enabling me to unlock this cleft from the ground.

That night, as we sat rather spiritlessly on the front steps after dinner, my sister began urging that he drive me twenty miles to the next town, which had a movie house. The idea amused her and Penelope can be foolishly insistent about anything which entertains her. Besides, she added, I must be bored and she needed to sleep for a while. I remember thinking she wanted to be rid of us for some reason, and while I was busy saying that I was not bored he went into the house and came back out with my sweater, the car keys, and a fresh bottle of beer.

We drove in the red truck, back to the same town I had arrived in by bus three days before. We sat beside one another in the movie theater, and in the semidarkness he began touching me. I will not defend myself. I was experiencing a peculiar revenge towards my sister. But I intended this familiarity to stop; I fully intended to control its limits.

Later, when he drove onto the dirt road which led to the graveyard, saying that he had left something, I knew that my revenge had conjoined with his and that we would very soon prove uncontrollably, weakly submissive to our instincts.

He parked behind the white shed, leaving the door of the truck yawning open. I sat a while in the cab before switching off the headlights. I was aware of the crisp keening of crickets, aware of my name being called.

The kerosene lamp was set perilously, I observed, on the wooden floor. The sleeping bag, with its gash of red lining, lay open beside it. Standing over the desk, I idly turned pages lit by the uncurtained window and the moon beyond. Here were names and dates of the dead and maps of the cemetery drawn in swooping lines of black ink. I could not imagine my name among these or my sister's name, or his. I turned then and said boldly that she had arranged all this. My sister managed everything for me, I told him.

Senseless husks of men and women lay face upwards all around us. A short time afterwards we dressed and drove aimlessly around the graveyard, the headstones flashing up like white filings in the noon glare of the headlights. Once he honked the horn and we laughed.

He went directly and with triumphant face to Penelope's room while I was left in the kitchen, surrounded by the pretty things which had always been hers. African violets bloomed feverishly in enameled pots. A stained-glass picture of an orange cat hunched around a sheaf of something, wheat perhaps or pussy willows, hung by a lead chain in the window. Penelope's cat came in and slouched against my leg, mistaking me for her until I jumped away from it. The refrigerator set up a mechanical drone; I saw a tombstone in its sleek white shape and thought my comparison quite funny.

I told myself as I walked, the sweet gumlike odor of the phlox clinging persistently to me, that I could return to my apartment. I could go back, full of childish confession, to the handsome, vacant priest. But I came here to this white shed, to its musty earth-burdened interior. And I find brief penance in this digging.

Lowering myself into the narrow bed, I settled damp, stained leaves over my body, put a small clod of dirt upon my tongue, and stared upwards, with the others, at the outflung, random stars.

There was an old woman called nothing-at-all,
Who rejoiced in her dwelling exceedingly small.
A man stretched his mouth to its utmost extent,
And down at one gulp house and old woman went.

Penelope found me by morning, heavy-bodied with cold, and hauling me half-up from where I had dug, she held me. My sister's wrenching beauty was put aside for my sake, and we were together. She continued to hold me until affection rose in us, fateful as our births, aching with grace.

Disturbing No One

Elsa Wagner navigated, leaving her feverish wake among the brightly preserved, gamy corpses of Rome, while her mother, a cloth laid over her eyes and ankles elevated, napped. She took a complicated series of buses to San Pietro in Vincoli to view *Moses* and the chains which had bound St. Peter. Elsa went in and out of dank, aphotic churches as quickly as if they were shops which did not carry the brand she insisted on.

Ingrid Toller was not unaware that her forty-two-year-old daughter, still handsome, and brainy in that unsensible way of aesthetes, was afflicted by a recurrent spiritual palsy, yet she had no clue as to the wild oscillations Elsa was beginning to make between the charged field of eroticism and the flat line of morbidity. While Mrs. Toller dozed in her silk slip, with instructions for the front desk to ring at four-thirty, her daughter dragged the stuff of her unlived selves like some bluish caul over the sundry, worn-down sights of Rome.

Ingrid and Elsa had toured what was mandatory: Vatican, Colosseum, Pantheon, Fountain of Trevi, Piazzas di Spagna, Navona. Elsa was patient as her mother bought up silk scarves, leather handbags, perfumes, glassware, giving over currency with the floppy ease that overlies deep wells of vaulted cash. At outdoor cafés they compressed enthusiasms upon the white backs of post-cards, Elsa addressing the *Pietà* to her husband, and *Venus Rising from the Sea* to each of her two high-school-aged sons. Weakening to her own mischief at one point, Ingrid sent picture postcards of Pope Paul VI to her husband and friends, saying Rome's male escort service was an awful letdown.

Ingrid Toller gave off a ruddy, hot look of boiled crustacean. She wore Lilly Pulitzer skirts with turtles or whales or frogs all over them; her purses were varnished tackle baskets trimmed with lime or raspberry grosgrain. She had no eye for understating her-self. When she spoke, her red, freckly arms waved about, seg-mented like a lobster's; in repose, her face resembled a balloon left behind the couch for a week. Her toes hurt; she could never find the perfect triple A, and she referred to her deadpan feet as drudgesome things, relations she could not shake off, literally, but owed something to.

As if in compensation, Elsa was tall, uncomplaining, subtly, classily pale, with blunt shoulder-length khaki hair. She ordered conservative pieces from the Talbot's catalogues, organized her wardrobe around taupe and wine, navy and camel. Elsa was visual understatement itself.

* * *

Their first afternoon in Rome, Elsa lay down, but her mother's stertorous bulk in the opposite bed was so vexing she put her low-heeled shoes back on, left a note, and exited their quiet hotel, her purse strapped across her chest to discourage thieves.

On her walk Elsa came upon the notorious ossuary of Ca-puchin monks. After paying a small fee, she was directed down a hall of gray stone with open chambers along its left flank. Each of the dozen or so chambers overflowed with a promiscuous jumble of bones. Skeletons of forty thousand Capuchin monks from the fourteenth to the nineteenth centuries, dismantled and reset into primitive mosaics . . . umbles and whorls of thigh bones, mush-

room-cap skulls, hips like bruised gardenia petals, all this grim
handiwork with monks' bones. And beneath glass, upon purple
tasseled cushions, lodged the blackened clumps of human hearts.

"Excuse me. Is there more?" At her question, a monk whose
oyster-colored face seemed pried from between its flanges of
brown cowl, pointed to the wall opposite the souvenir shop.
There was a large sign on its otherwise blank expanse, the words
repeated in a dozen languages:

Once We Were Like You.
One Day You Will Be
Like Us.

* * *

Over dinner at La Rampa, Ingrid decided that Elsa had displayed something less than good taste, staying in such a grisly
place, much less inquiring to see more.

"Religion, taken too far," she said, "turns people fanatic, Elsa.
And fanatics have *no* aesthetic sense. It creates a vicious half-
circle."

"Yes, Mother, but fanatics are the only ones not washed away
by time. Excessive temperaments stand out in history. In order to
hold the attention of future generations, you need to murder
enormous numbers of people. Order a Colosseum made on the
flayed backs of slaves. Be Michelangelo. Be a genius with ego and
say no to the Pope. Be the Pope. Behave as if magnified a thousand times over."

"You are saying only the most flagrant action endures?"

"It's what interests us, isn't it? We carry guidebooks, buy maps
which lead us to the results of excess. The distance of history morally numbs us to the acts of Caesar; he ends up impressing us."

Ingrid wasn't listening, she was over-paying a gypsy girl for
two long-stem roses. She turned back brightly to Elsa.

"I'm going to have the penne alla vodka; our waiter recom-
mends it. And for you, Elsa dear, two Roman roses . . . because

I'm so pleased we could chuck our boys for a bit, have this adventure to ourselves."

* * *

Rome's buses were claustrophobic tumbrels whose passengers were stacked and flung like rendered sheep. Elsa, her hand gripping a chrome bar, was pressed against a variety of bodies, but determined to find her way, without taxi, to San Pietro in Vincoli. All at once she felt a subtle, deliberate push against her backside. Through the thin, expensive challis of her Talbot's skirt, she felt the bulgy gob of a penis nudge between her buttocks. She thought of a cigar, dropped between the raised lips of an ashtray. Then she thought, this must be a mistake, an absentmindedness on somebody's part. She could not bring herself to turn and look at her assailant, but at the next stop, as more people plunged onto the bus, Elsa shifted and repositioned herself. And though she had moved, she felt it again, the unmistakable plug of a half-erect penis. Such mean anonymity, when she was wedged in and could not possibly move. At the next stop, Elsa fought her way out, trembling, to the sidewalk. She hiked up a number of hills, narrowing like steep perspectives, until she reached the yellow church which held Michelangelo's *Moses* and St. Peter's chains.

Elsa did not pray in these churches she invaded. She tried in the first, but it was a costive, puny effort. When walking past the skeletons of monks, Elsa may have aimed for some form of spiritual reverie, but really, what she mourned was the slippage of her own life, the piecemeal loss of her looks. Women did not bother with her face anymore, though they glanced appraisingly at the expense and quality of her clothing. Older, fastidious men eyed her not with the lust she might have liked, but with admiration and guarded potency.

She walked, arriving late at their hotel. Ingrid, in a geranium-splashed dress, sat in a blue striped chair in the lobby, chatting with an attorney and his wife from Ohio. God, her mother could and did talk to anyone.

At dinner, as Elsa described her public assault, Ingrid's sympathy was curbed. "Money, Elsa, serves in part to elevate you above such experiences. It isn't sensible, risking insult in that way. Taking the public bus invites danger. It's nearly as bad as walking alone at night, for heaven's sake."

* * *

On their last full day in Rome, Mrs. Toller and her daughter returned to the Vatican. Elsa skimmed the artwork, keeping a distracted eye out for Mother Teresa, whom their concierge had claimed was in Rome. Going into a pink marble chapel, Elsa saw four nuns in pale blue saris. A sign said Service for World Peace. One of the shrouded figures praying aloud in Hindi was Mother Teresa, Elsa was convinced, yet the nuns' faces were swallowed in the fluted lips of saris. Was it a sign she should recognize, that she and Mother Teresa were here at the same time? Elsa tried diligently to pray for world peace.

Ingrid was not enamored of the Polish nun. Wasn't *she,* as a wife and mother, in involuntary servitude, a sad result of sexist distortions? Only now, with her children grown, her husband's fortune secure, could she pursue or identify her own interests. Mother Teresa, with her conservative exhortations to women, hardly seemed in step. It was saintly enough, this work with the dying, the poor. But, Ingrid complained, leave us modern, ordinary women alone.

* * *

As Elsa's religious self surfaced, nourished in the potent, etherous Catholicism of Rome, so did its surprise twin, lust. Hitting hardest, this free-floating lust, in hotel rooms. The sensuality of dimmed, vacated space, the dominant placement of beds where nothing personal existed, no familiar imprint to blunt the raw edge. The man on the bus, pressing himself against her, she wanted his sort of sex in the blank chilly caves of hotel rooms.

Of course, when her mother stepped into those places, all was immediately spoiled. Lights were flicked on, suitcases snapped open, the business of hanging clothing, placing out cosmetics, things strewn and piled about, banal conversation, all went into smashing Elsa's erotic, broody state of mind. It was in those purer moments, when she was given a key to inspect the room, or when her mother stepped out for something or took a long, quiet bath . . .

Throughout her adult life, Elsa had avoided scandal. Had never been sexually indiscreet. Had earned that worldly benefit of morality, an untarnished social prestige. Deliberately, she had undermined her interest in men, certainly in sex. Now, in Rome, and why she couldn't say, Elsa Wagner was being made physically weak by the sight of male bodies. She craved passing men the way her mother coveted expensive objects behind shop windows. Very young men drew her eye, which shamed her. Was it Rome, its decadent remnants, its lavish, undraped statuary? Its young men? (Repeatedly, she fixed on languid Raphael types, elongated feminine faces, greyhound leanness of limb, repelled by the bluntheaded types, who brought to mind bullish emperors stamped onto rough coins.)

Only in churches, among corpses of saints, among Americans earnestly examining history as it collapsed about them, and with so little discrimination that as a national group they looked exhausted and peevish (did they seek, with her, some common shelter?) . . . only in the dark sleep of churches could Elsa dodge her own alarming appetites.

* * *

On the train (because Elsa wanted this last-minute detour, hoping Assisi, clean, as a place of pilgrimage, might somehow help), Ingrid hardly bothered looking out the window of their first-class compartment. She circled her puffy ankles, leaned her head into moss velvet upholstery, shut her eyes.

"So, Elsa, what was your impression of the Eternal City?"

Picking my way across a sprawl of corpse, scuttling over its clefts of rot, feasting on its huge, graying bloat . . .

"It was more beautiful than I expected, Mother."

Elsa was looking at the countryside. Pink chips of houses, tiled roofs, ivy-green shutters. Vineyards, vegetable plots, chicken coops. Acres of blackened sunflowers, uncut, heads like scorched, bent spoons. She had no idea why they were like that.

She saw two big women, tamped down into heavy skirts, bursting from blouses, red kerchiefs on their ball-like heads, heaving things up from the soil. Roots, cabbages? She wanted to show these Brueghel-like creatures to her mother, but the drawback to rapid travel was everything slewing past before you could elaborate or confirm. You could say lamely, "I saw the most amazing thing just now," but it would be like a botched punch line.

By late afternoon they'd come to the walled hill town of Assisi. Ingrid settled at an outdoor café with her bar of chocolate and an English newspaper, scanning headlines about a second terrorist bombing on the train run from Rome to Florence. Elsa, starting with the two highest-rated hotels, worked her way down, finally finding a vacant room above a trattoria for eight dollars. Taking a key up the pinched, turning stairs, she unlocked the door and met with a room so frugal it physically pained her. A crucifix hung between thin, lumpy beds no better than cots. Her erotic impulses must have been some aberration of Rome, some side effect not uncommon to travelers temporarily unspoused.

She experienced little in this room but relief.

✷ ✷ ✷

Elsa scrunched down so that she could lie in the high-shouldered, basin-sized tub and turn the waxy pages of a little booklet about St. Francis. Clammy, toadish water belled over her stomach. When she came out from the tiny bathroom, her mother was folded on her side as though she were an amulet carefully stored in a box. Elsa felt a chest-clot of affection for her mother. Shopkeepers adored her. So did hotel people. She lightened their monotonous work, was generous, garrulous with them. Unlike Elsa, embedded in peculiar solitude, the sort of tourist who gets under the skin of sales and hotel people. The type aching to understand humanity but buying nothing.

Ingrid had been resilient about their sparse room. "This will be good for us. Absolutely appropriate, to deprive ourselves in the village of a saint. A lovely idea, Elsa." She pronounced Assisi charming, naif, was already plotting which native potteries to buy. She would purchase a dozen at least of the smaller size rooster pitchers. Grand bridge and hostess gifts.

One night's self-denial had tested Ingrid and Elsa sufficiently. By early morning they were seated on an elegant terrace of the Subasio Hotel, paying twice what their night's lodging had cost for bread and pots of bitter coffee.

Elsa devised the day's excursion. Ingrid should see the Basilica of San Francisco, but briefly; overlong exposure to miracles, saints, blown-up virtue of any sort would make her mother restive, damp her enjoyment. Elsa would go on alone to the Church of Santa Chiara, walk the path down to the Convent of San Damiano. They would meet for lunch, pack, then catch the bus down to the station in Santa Maria degli Angeli. Leave on the four o'clock train for Venice.

At clipped pace they toured the Basilica, its upper and lower churches, the saint's crypt, the Sienese frescoes. The Giotto frescoes. They stood before Francis's sandals, his robe, a note he had scrawled to a close friend, Brother Elia. In this presence of saint's things, Elsa felt visceral shiftings, like the subtle swim of geographic plates. She believed the life of Francis, like that of Mother Teresa, was the truest life; her own, a job lot of overlapping loyalties, fickle intent, her convictions diluted by what surrounded and seemed to most need her. She lacked the will to act without compromise.

Elsa persisted, walking through the village, to the Church of Santa Chiara, climbing downstairs to the vault she had read about in the bathtub, to see the body of St. Claire, face upwards, hands stiffened in prayer, and, like Snow White, set into a crystal coffin. This grotesque, mummified remain, on its mattress of gold, had established the sister order to Francis's little brothers. Poor Claires, wasn't that it? In nun's habit, black netting propped over the carious black face as if to keep pieces from flying upwards . . . Elsa shuddered, went upstairs to a side chapel, looked at the painted cross that had spoken to Francis.

GO FRANCIS, AND REPAIR MY CHURCH, WHICH,
AS YOU SEE, IS FALLING INTO RUIN.

Elsa needed to repair herself, reduce her own selfishness, join a lay order of some sort, adopt a child from Nicaragua or Cambodia. Humanitarian intentions pelted through her. But her family, what would they think? Surely they would tease or object. Turning to leave, Elsa saw an area screened off by an elaborate grillwork. She went over to it, looked in, saw a woman's red cloak, a Bible, various personal articles on display. Seated on a diminutive chair, in the midst of these relics, a child-sized nun rose up fluid as air, came to stand before her. Will you hear the story of our Santa Chiara? Elsa nodded. The nun's voice was intimate and empty, her face veiled once by cloth and masked once again behind iron grillwork. She spoke in hypnotic, accented English about the merchant's daughter with golden hair, gesturing to a shank of saint's hair, pinned blatant and worldly to the otherwise bare wall. A young woman giving up wealth and social position to live out the ideals of her childhood companion, Francis. Elsa suspected the nun of rubbing the truth from this fairy tale. The stem of red-gold curling hair cried false from its wall. This tale of virtue was fabrication. Claire and Francis had obviously been in love. When Francis, swarmed upon by God, renounced earthly longings, including Claire, she said that if he would have God Alone, then so would she. So. The romance had been plucked from this story. Any fool could guess how Francis had kissed Claire, how they met by night in the olive groves . . . how Claire must have raised their illegitimate child within the cloister. Elsa was feeling giddy. The nun stopped, sat down until the next tourist appeared and she could float, wraithlike, up to the grill.

Elsa took the sloping footpath down through dusty olive orchards, hundreds of dwarfed knotty trees with coarse grass spiking around their bases. She toured Claire's convent, San Damiano. The rooms were shrunken, had the wet smell of unlit stone. The touted frugality seemed sensual to Elsa. Most rooms had tiny windows, and out those windows, like cut jewels, flashed gold fields, hillsides, deep sky, the dark scatter of birds.

. . . Droning at her, these gray humps of stone, the bulk and heft of timbers. The refectory was cramped. She hiked back up the footpath, entered the cobbled village, out of breath, extremely hungry, light-headed.

And found her mother easily, spotted the bright whaleprint skirt. Standing with a pair of shopkeepers who had the look of people clobbered by good luck. She must have bought out their roosters.

Elsa stopped, bought postcards, then, strangely fascinated, watched Ingrid. Her mother took prescribed pills at mealtime. She grew short of breath. One day Ingrid Toller would be rived from her money, from the shops in which to spend it, would be moved quietly, with tasteful ceremony, onto the topmost layer of human history. A smear of topsoil upon fathoms of humus. Then it would be Elsa's turn. Both of them taken into the earth, breathed in, like billions before them.

One Day You Will Be
Like Us.

Elsa stood in the street, under the hot Italian sun, stripped, dizzied, thinking what she needed was food. Thinking how silly, this early grief.

She walked, wanting to catch up with her mother, unsure how to present this awkward, unchanged baggage, herself. Departing life bit by bit. Holding the pendulum's staff, death the steady swing. This person who would never define herself further than her own death. Still lovely, the flesh, thoughts, and instincts of

Elsa Wagner, though in fewer and fewer lights could any of them sustain inspection.

Oh! What a source of cohesion and cowardice, family bonds!

"Mother! My God, what have you bought now? I'm absolutely starved. I could eat a Roman cat. Where shall we go?"

"I just asked the darling people at the shop back there. They recommend this little place, out of the way, very untouristy. And we shouldn't miss the veal."

Mrs. Toller and her daughter asked directions and before long were conversing through a superb lunch, served in a walled garden, anticipating the next step of their trip through Italy. Venice.

Dutifully they wrote their postcards, Elsa with this doggish sense of betrayal (to that spectral self folding and unfolding out of darkened, tenebrous churches?), as she wrote:

Assisi a charming village, home of
St. Francis . . . you remember, dears,
the saint wearing birds on his shoulders
and squirrels for slippers? Always my
favorite saint. Grandma and I off to
Venice. Home in ten days. Time flies.
Miss you all. Love, Mother

With trained, conscientious habit, Elsa thus bent her head to her task, at once tightening and submitting to the family bond.

Disturbing no one.

A Man Around the House

I suspected him the minute he parked his suitcase on our front porch, hearing him ask Mercy, who stood behind the screen door, if this was the Three Sisters Shelter for the Aged and Retired. From where I sat, in deep shade, in my wheelchair, I could see that the handkerchief he wiped over his face was soiled and that the socks he wore did not match, one being tan, the other black. But Mercy couldn't see that. She pushed open the door and let him step inside our farmhouse. In my opinion, that was the most ignorant thing she could have done.

Elwynn Coombs planted himself like a lily inside our house. During supper he sat with Mercy and my younger sister, Clothilde, over plates of boiled ham, creamed corn, and orange Jello salad. Clo giggled and snapped her fingers at every other thing he said; Mercy cut her piece of ham into small squares, chewed her food, and said nothing. I sat with the others at the card table by the open window. Once in a while I reached across the table and with a paper napkin wiped corn that strayed from Mr. Simmons' mouth. Worse than feeding babies, I thought. Babies have appetite.

Mrs. Ellish, forking oleo into a dish of noodles, knocked over her cup of weak tea. Her voice had loosened up and gone bad; it vibrated like she was being shaken up and down. "Fumble fingers," she sighed.

Henry Flock smirked. Between meals he keeps to his bedroom, where he sits under a reading lamp, holding a green plastic flyswatter. During meals he recalls a girlfriend he had in San Francisco when he was a young man, and that usually cheers him up.

Not one other person has come here in three years. Mercy says it's because the sign we put up on the highway is washed out from the stress of facing south. We've no reputation. She mentioned getting the sign touched up or replaced, but she'd never bothered with it. She doesn't do much except tinker with broken-down machinery in the barn.

When Elwynn Coombs asked if he could stay on another day or so, Mercy was so anxious to pay off our debts that she reached and grabbed the check he wrote out to her. I recall that his handwriting made me queasy. No man worth his salt writes with such fat female letters. And my sister Clo never did have nerve enough to turn down strays of any variety, so there Coombs sat, flipping through a magazine, sucking up the coffee she brought him, and picking his teeth for relaxation. Clothilde's skin, which is usually the tone of soya flour, due to anemia and bile, blared an unnatural red in his presence, which meant that her circulation was still good, among other things.

With Pappa's black Sunday hat on my head for shade, I sat on the porch next morning, witnessing Clothilde and that Elwynn Coombs character walk out to the flower garden. It had been our mother's garden, square and colorful, with an oyster shell path cutting down the middle. Pappa had bought arched white trellises—"bridal bowers," he'd called them—to set at either end of the path. Now they are being dragged down, at varying angles, by the vigorous honeysuckle. Clo was proud of the flower garden, as she had worked it back from a nearly wild, decayed state.

I observed that Coombs fellow, knee-deep among the white

phlox, coreopsis, daylilies, and blue monkshood, polite as a printed invitation, his hands clasped behind his back. Clothilde stooped down to yank at a weed, and he looked back at the house for a moment, studying it. Clo straightened herself up; he tugged at a flower and handed her the broken-off part.

They had to bend down together to get through the collapsing trellis, and they walked back up to the house, Clo waving the drooping flower in her hand. Her face was red and her red hair had struggled out from the knot at the back of her neck. They came slowly up the steps.

Mr. Coombs' blue and white striped shirt had crescents of wet under the arms. I guessed then he was at least twenty-five years younger than Clo, but not much healthier. He had purplish gray pouches under his eyes; his hair was damp and slick like thin yellow grass, and it broke across his forehead so that he kept wiping it back with his hand. When he saw me, he made a stiff little bow and was about to speak when Clo explained that I was part-paralyzed by stroke. With a giggle, she asked him inside the house for a glass of buttermilk.

Around noontime Mercy trotted up from the barn, sat on the front steps, and drank from a glass of sweet tea Clo had set out for her. She was wearing father's old work clothes, the greasy trousers and the gray shirt with the ripped pocket. From the back, with her hair clipped so short, you could mistake her for a man. All three of us used to have the same red hair. The color is drained off from mine now. My hair was once so long and heavy that I could wrap it around a fencepost with enough left to tie into a bowknot.

From inside the house I heard Elwynn Coombs and Clothilde laughing. Mercy heard them too as she slammed her work boots against the steps and bits of mud flew off. The back of her shirt had a sweat stain like a yoke or maybe a pair of wings across the shoulders.

"I don't like that Mr. Coombs much," she said. "I tell myself he's all right. I tell myself he's a blessing. He's here, I say, so we can pay off some debts. I hope Clothilde has lunch prepared. Mr. Simmons didn't touch his egg this morning. Again. He wastes things."

The screen door banged shut behind her.

After lunch, Coombs stretched himself out on the horsehair sofa in the front room, snoring, a newspaper peaked over his face. Supper persuaded him back to a vertical position. He sat across from Mercy and Clothilde, hungrily piling sliced beets and cold chicken onto his plate, his jaw swiveling and grinding exactly like a horse's, until Mercy said, "Just what is it that you do, Mr. Coombs?"

"Salesman," he said through a mouthful of food, which he sluiced down with milk. Clothilde fluttered her fingers oddly and dipped her fork in and out of the pieces of food on her plate, leaving most of them uneaten.

"What is it that you sell, Mr. Coombs?" asked Mercy.

"Well," he grinned, "that all depends. I've got to be a judge of character. Take the time I saw you, behind the screen door, I figured you to be easy bait for my set of encyclopedias. A type that's after facts, I told myself. Your sister, she's got unusual tastes. She would be leaning to art, beauty, things of that sort. She would be a dead ringer for my jewelry collection." He winked at Clothilde.

I wiped a string of beet juice off Mr. Simmons' chin. Apparently Mr. Coombs had not bothered to judge my character.

"Books and trinkets, then," Mercy said shortly. She picked up the milk pitcher and came over to our table.

Coombs shrugged and poked another forkful of chicken into his mouth. Clothilde scraped the beets from her plate back onto the serving dish.

"When she died, Mother left us some fine old jewelry which we have not yet . . ."

"Please, Clothilde." Mercy stopped pouring and glared at her sister. I happened to be watching Mr. Elwynn Coombs, particularly around the eyes, with that vivid light in them. I reminded myself what Jesus himself said, Judge not unless you be so judged, isn't that right?

So Mercy sat down and asked him, point-blank, where his books and jewelry were. After all, he had brought only a small suitcase with him. And as a matter of fact, as long as she was a type for facts and for gathering facts together, his striped shirt from that morning was washed and laid over the porch railing to dry, and he was only wearing a damp undershirt to dinner.

"Sold everything," he yelped proudly. "I'm on my way back to the city day after tomorrow, on Saturday, to get a fresh supply of goods. Clothes included. I'm a rich man, ladies." He wiped his hair back from his forehead.

But if he was a rich man, except for one bank check with that fat loopy signature of his, I hadn't seen any sign of it.

He stayed on the next day, too, lolling on the sofa, reading newspapers which weren't even up to date as our subscription had run out. When he sensed she was anxious about him, he handed Mercy another one of his fancy checks, which she carefully folded and put into a glass canning jar on the kitchen shelf.

My other sister, Clo, turned herself inside out for Elwynn Coombs. At one point I found her in the hall, in front of the full-length mirror, with him standing behind her, showing with his hands where a brooch would set off her blouse. She was flirting with him, and I was so ashamed for her I wheeled myself right past as if neither of them were there.

Mercy worried about him too, but we let him stay. That was our mistake, figuring he'd be gone soon and we'd be the better for it. We'd have our bills paid. Besides, worthless as he behaved, he was a young man, and it affected all of us, particularly Clothilde, to whom he paid the most complimentary attention.

We all have duties here. Saturday breakfast I came to the dining room, finding it empty except for sunlight, and no food being prepared in the kitchen. Clothilde's supposed to wake our residents, help

them dress for the day and get them into the dining room. I wheeled
down the hallway to the residents' rooms and pushed open the first
door. There was Mercy, helping Henry Flock struggle into his shirt
and trousers.

"Your sister's gone off," Mercy snapped. "Wake up Mr.
Coombs and ask him to please boil up some eggs instead of eating
half a dozen for a change. We are behind schedule."

I went along and pushed open Mr. Coombs' door. The edges of
the curtains hung still. The bed was poorly made, the blanket
yanked up over the pillow. Mr. Coombs and his suitcase were
gone.

Mercy calmly fixed up a breakfast, then put through a call for
help. He was picked up within an hour, hitchhiking with his little
beat-up suitcase full of Mamma's jewelry and several other things
besides. And Coombs wasn't his right name at all. It was Elmore
Stevens.

The sheriff and his assistant drove onto our property to see if
Clothilde had returned home yet. Mercy said no, she hadn't, but
thank Jesus she hadn't been foolish enough to run off with that
character. She asked the officers if they wouldn't like a swallow of
something or a plate of food, but they both said thank you, no,
and the sheriff said in a low voice that they'd just start what they
came for and take a look around the property.

The woods will be the place, I thought. Check the woods first.
That's where she'll have gone to.

Clothilde returned home in the hottest part of the afternoon,
when the freshness is burned off the garden and the sky and the
land itself. I had set my wheelchair in the shade of the clematis
vine which has star-like purple blossoms and not much scent. I
saw Mercy come hopping down the steps and run over to the two
men who held her sister in their arms. I guessed they had found
her in that damned woodlot, in the one last piece of uncut land
around here.

I've never cared for wildness in the land. A person's business, like the Bible instructs, is to subdue the land, put up a fence around it, and make it meet your gaze. I never cared for that woodlot.

Her thin auburn hair swung this way and that as they carried her up to the porch; the way it bumped against the steps reminded me of our childhood's rhymes. Her eyes were shut, her neck ugly and swollen, a lavender chain of Michaelmas asters circled her wrist.

The officers brought her into the house, Mercy holding open the door. A wasp lighted on my sleeve; I knocked at it and missed. After that I let it wander stupidly across the flower pattern of my dress, hunting for nourishment.

They took her to her old room until Mr. Diehl, the undertaker from town, could come out the next day. I agreed with Mercy that she would be buried right beside Mamma and Pappa in the Presbyterian churchyard down the road.

Mercy sat on the horsehair sofa, answering the sheriff's questions. She gave over the phony checks. She spoke on the phone twice with Mr. Diehl, and she welcomed the minister and his wife who drove up to offer assistance. I kept watch outside Clothilde's room, wanting and not wanting to open the door and see her stretched out on her bed with the pink chenille spread, picturing whatever the dead may picture.

I hope she had some happiness before he killed her anyway.

Mercy went down to the barn after the officers left, and I went out on the porch at sunset, to see her driving around the pasture in Pappa's old tractor, going in smaller and tighter circles until she stopped and just sat there, probably blaming herself.

The minister's wife had gone home and come back with a casserole for our residents. I sat at the card table cleaning off Mr. Simmons' face while Mr. Flock recalled a girlfriend in San Francisco when he was in the Navy, and Clara Ellish, in her failing voice, pursued a repetitive, dissolving melody.

I thought about how most lives start with clear-eyed dreaming and finish when the eyes are exhausted and muddied with memory. And through the middle, disappointment springing up colorless, like wild grass, tough and deep rooted.

With Clothilde it had been different. Nothing passed by to make Clothilde stop dreaming.

I remind Mercy, as I follow her about the dark narrowing farmhouse, that our sister Clothilde gave up her life partly because it was the first time we'd had a healthy and vigorous man around the house, since Pappa, in a long, troublesome while.

Dead Finish

Heat dulls the village. Pigs and dogs alike, tongues flagged, hides rimed with dust, burrow under the pilings of thatched houses. Grief too dulls the village, damping voices to the torpid revolve of the long-bodied wasp in its season. Winter. *Invierno.*

Families line up, dressed in church clothes, before the drowned boy's house. The older sisters come down the steps to pass wooden bowls of cigarettes and betel leaf, betel nut. Mourners go inside, walk around the cleanly clothed body (white shirt, dark trousers, hair so deftly arranged you can see ridge marks the wetted comb has made). They are respectful, the mourners, chewing on the betel, exhaling smoke with dignified restraint. The mother and father, grandparents and younger children sit on the left-hand side of the body. Their faces, amber stones along strands of greenish smoke, are blankly ceremonial.

The almost dreamy procession keeps on as Dr. Grimmen, his wife, Augusta, and eight-year-old son, Alex, drive up in a black Model T. They get out, stand uncertainly near the car, as if for protection. Dr. and Mrs. Grimmen look uneasy but determined.

With trained politeness, they refuse the cigarettes, the betel leaf not really intended for them.

At first they place themselves at the end of the line, the doctor an almost freakish height among the villagers, his eyeglasses floating like twin remote lagoons in the center of a face occult as drought. His wife is small-boned like the villagers, but her hair, the color of blood meal, is crimped like shrimps' tails, and her skin, like coconut meat, is very white. Their son, his hair pale as an angel's, eats his fingernails, scuffs his good foot in the dust. The smaller foot balances him, the calf of the leg mute, gyved in its leather-and-metal brace.

Some lengthy minutes pass before Dr. Grimmen steers his wife by the elbow and his son by the nape of the neck, removing his family from the line and ushering them up the steps into the hut. When the Doctor emerges he looks grave, relieved at having done his duty. Mrs. Grimmen follows, a handkerchief pressed to her mouth, a result of the greenish smoke, the tragic sight of her housekeeper's boy. Alex blinks in the tropical glare. He does not walk beside his father, whom he blames, or his mother, whose confused sympathies he is ashamed of.

The Grimmens drive out of the village, dust drawing up pillars behind them. They drive back to Agana.

When the noise of the car, its modern machinery, has faded, sound breaks from the hut, sound like bone cracked in the jaws of a dog, sound that turns into a stringy series of yawps. To the guests outside, many with lips and teeth looking bloodsmeared from the betel juice, that sound, the mother's sound, comes as the one exhalation of wind in a hot oppression of air.

DR. GRIMMEN   AGANA   1926

If I admit to Gusty that he puked, I'll never unhook him. Ever since his polio, she's had Alex pinned under a damn bell jar. Stunting him.

First he balls his fists into his eyes. Then ducks his head and whimpers. That was when I'd had enough. I forced him to watch a cockfight for what it was, native sport, pure as baseball. In rebellion, I presume, he puked. Alex was longjawed, miserable on the ride home. At one point he spoke up, saying if he had a rooster he'd keep it with his other pets, not make it fight and be killed. What in God's name would happen, son, if everybody reasoned as you do, if every living creature was sentenced to be someone's house pet? We'd end up like Hindus, starving right alongside our cows. Oh well. So what have you got at the present time, son? A pack of house-lizards, a couple of fruit doves, and a half-wild pony? What have I forgotten?

His first faint smile. My blue-tailed skink.

Right. Your blue-tailed skink. Those are supposed to be symbols of good luck around here.

I know.

By then we were back home, Gusty waiting near the breadfruit tree in our yard, looking worried—and very lovely.

Now remember, son, we had a good time. That is all your mother needs to hear.

ALEX GRIMMEN   1972

When I first met *chamorros,* as the native people of Guam are called, I thought their faces like butterflies, with a dark line of quiet dropping down the center. Not so much quiet as indifference. When they'd gently reach out to my hair, rare because of its uncolored whiteness, even their curiosity had some deep fault or split of apathy sunk down its middle. Father used to say *chamorros* did not possess the modern temperament. Imagine, he'd say, measuring distance by how many cigarettes a man has to smoke to get from one spot to another. That sort of substitute for thinking baffled and often enough aggravated my father, whose own mind was mapped as precisely as a graph.

That Sunday afternoon Father took me to the cockfight a defined excitement was swelling the faces of the *chamorros;* still, there was that cold dead stripe between the eyes, as though they understood the fate of cocks and of themselves to be eventually the same. But, crowded into the shaded amphitheater of nipa palm, bamboo, and coconut thatch, they could watch it happen, gamble on the outcome, find sport in the process, something they would hardly be willing to do upon the occasion of their own deaths.

Father and I got on fairly well until he formed the resolution to change me. Perhaps it was anger at the polio for having left me asymmetrical, imperfect. Mother responded to my crisis by becoming overprotective. She no longer trusted nature. Father coped by pushing me past my capacities.

My temperament, both before and after the polio, was solitary and somewhat unambitious. Now those tendencies, coupled with the sight of my leg brace, seemed to exasperate Father, to trip his patience. I idled over books, fooled with my geckos, named "island canaries" because of their insistent, high-pitched chirp, talked to the fruit doves perched in their two-storied bamboo cage. I brushed and rode my pony. I had made no especially close friends. We had been in Guam nearly eight months when Father informed Mother and me that he was resolved to train and strengthen my weak body and threatened character.

The cockfight was his first, his clumsiest idea, and it went badly. My heart was all for the poor birds, hauled into the dirt pit of the amphitheater, their owners seizing their plumed tails so each bird would scratch and pull toward the other in a display of supposed fierceness. I remember the noisy hurl of money into the pit, along with much shouting, the attendant raking up coins and paper money before setting two cocks in the pit, one dark, the other white, each with a steel gaff on its leg. Disembowelment was sudden. Throughout the afternoon the pit and much of the money became bloodsprayed.

I protested by refusing to look, until Father grabbed the hair at the back of my head, pulling hard so I had to look. It's for your own good, time you came down off your mother's lap, he said, or some such hurtful nonsense. I answered soon enough, by being sick to my stomach.

On the ride home he was partly didactic, partly silent, altogether distracted, pressed to think up some better way to exercise my character. This may have been when he hit upon the idea of a friendship with the housekeeper's son. It was not long after the cockfight that I was introduced to Paul.

DOCTOR GRIMMEN   1926

Gusty and I are equally hopeful when the housekeeper's boy arrives in pressed shirt, neat pants, his hair so deftly groomed you can see ridge marks from the wetted comb. He acts a bit hangdog with us, but soon enough sidles into Alex's room where the boys will have to be coaxed out for lunch on the verandah. When his mother is ready to leave, late in the day, both boys appear regretful. Alex's manner especially suggests that most treasured aspect of childhood, having a conspirator, a confidant one's own age.

ALEX   1972

In his village, two miles inland from Agana, Paul came to be envied as the boy invited every Sunday to the Navy doctor's house. My friend would return to his village late on those days with his mother, set apart by uneasy privilege.

His loyalty to me seemed even to surpass the awe he must have felt in our home with its English china, its silver tea service used each afternoon at four o'clock, its ifilwood floors which his mother kept polished with coconut grated and wound into soft cloth, its vases made from the buttery joints of thorny bamboo and kept filled with exotic flowers, its darkened bedrooms, the high, hospital-like metal beds draped with sultanic lengths of mosquito netting, their gleaming legs stuck into tins of kerosene to keep centipedes and scorpions from climbing up . . .

For my part, I could not have conjured a better companion than Paul. We took turns bareback riding my pony, Babe, a shaggy puckish animal that trotted a good deal faster on its way into the stable than out. In my room we'd lie on our stomachs playing with the geckos, dropping moths and mosquitoes into their dry hasps of mouths, handling the callused file of their skin. Sometimes we would find six-inch centipedes with dark red or dark green scales overlapping like a shrimp's but so tough the heel of a shoe could not crush them. Paul used to come to the theater with me to see Charlie Chaplin and Buster Keaton movies. He was at our house the time Mother won an old touring car in the church raffle; as she was proudly steering the car up to our house, the engine, entirely rusted, fell out onto the road. That was a big laugh.

We spent less time at the house after Father began to take us motoring around the Island in Blackbird, our Model T. The official reason for those jaunts was to inspect naval first-aid stations; this Father did with intelligence and thoroughness, qualities which marked his entire career. On the way home from those inspections, there would often be a treat for Paul and me, usually a swim in one of Guam's shallow, reefed lagoons.

My father relished these outings. Coasting in our Model T down roads of crushed white coral, he would lead us in singing "Bye, Bye Blackbird" and something called "I Found a Million-Dollar Baby in the Five-and-Ten-Cent Store." Paul's and my favorite was this goofy Ogden Nash sort of piece. God knows where Father picked it up, but we would hang out of his car windows, bellowing like dry, maddened caraboas:

Oh the monkeys have no tails in
Zamboango

Oh the monkeys have no tails in
Zamboango
Oh the monkeys have no tails,
They were bitten off by snails . . .
Oh the monkeys have no tails in
Zamboango

(I discovered in an atlas recently that Zamboang*a* is a black fleck of island off the Philippines. I had always assumed it didn't exist.)

It began subtly enough, Father's engineering a contest between us. With a paternalism typical in those days of Americans towards the people of Guam, Father gave the broad hint to Paul, no malice intended, that the superior swimmer would be me.

He chose swimming (water the element my leg could most deceive itself in); it was a skill he had taught me while on board the *Gold Star,* our Navy transport out of Annapolis. Once each day I would remove the brace, lower myself into the wooden, canvas-lined pool, the cold slap of stale sea murk. In Guam these lessons were continued on Saturday mornings at nearby Piti Beach. Paul, by contrast, was a complacent swimmer; he revolved and dove naturally. He owned no sense of competition.

On Saturdays, Father timed me for speed and swiftness in my stroke, standing calf-deep in the water, a broad woven hat of pandanus leaf on his head, squinting at his stopwatch. Probably after I'd outstripped his modest expectations, the notion of competition, or contest, took ambitious root in him.

DR. GRIMMEN   AGANA
JANUARY 1927

What earthly good, my sitting here . . . Alex's face buckled into a pillow, his body fixed with loss and blame.

Life is a tragic thing, Alex. I learned that in Madison, in medical school. First thing they taught us. You are not gods. Things take place

in the body no medical skills can cure. Seems life sometimes likes to shake
up the arrogant bunch of us. Paul's heart was defective somehow, either
congenitally or the result of some early illness. Rheumatic fever, per-
haps. He strained during the race and boom. That was that. A thing
none of us could have predicted or prevented.

What earthly good, saying these things, but I say them anyway
if only to deflect the accusation coming off the boy like sweat. He
won't say it, though it's all he's thinking about. If I hadn't wanted
that race, if I hadn't pushed Alex to win, Paul, in trying to keep
up, might not have died.

I am haunted by images of my son, hop-running, his brace off,
the useless left foot flumping against sand as he stays beside his
friend, carried up from the water . . . kneeling on the other side
of Paul's face as I blow air into the salt-rimed mouth. Paul, face
down in the back seat of the car, Alex trying to climb over the seat
to get to him.

And Gusty, her sympathies misplaced, her conjectures an irri-
tant, because Alex has promised he will not upset his mother further with the full story or its details.

And I sit beside this boy whose heart has been broken—by his
father's medicine.

ALEX   1972

Father had Paul and me worked up over the race idea. He
promised a silver dollar to the winner; the loser could challenge
the following Sunday. It was to be an ongoing competition then,
and we saw our way to earning fortunes.

He gave us our choice of racetrack, as he called it, the lagoon at
Piti, shallow, safe as a baby's nursery, or the narrow cliffside beach
at Talago Bay, some twelve miles south. Paul and I were both avid
for Talago; Horsehead Bay we'd named this place with its gnarled
coral outcrops looking like primitive heads of horses with peaked,
sea-marbled manes.

Mother planned to accompany us, then stayed home. She had one of her tropical headaches, caused by the moist oppressive heat, particularly bad in the winter season.

On reaching Talago, Father brought out his trappings, the pandanus leaf hat, the stopwatch, the silverplate whistle. I thought he had never seemed in a livelier mood. Paul and I hopped about, shivering—like two fighting cocks, I remember thinking, one dark, the other light. I told Paul this, and we crowed in gargled voices, strutted and flapped arms, silly with excitement. The race would be to the farthest coral horsehead, just out to the reef and back. Father said it should take us under ten minutes each direction.

In those final minutes before my father's whistle, I began to feel some anxiety. It was clear he expected me to win, to confirm certain things he needed to believe about me, about us, and though Paul and I were closely matched as swimmers, he had grafted onto me the will to win, a thing no one had bothered to instill in my friend. It was, then, an unfair race.

Paul and I shook hands, formally. We separated at the edge of the bay, walking into water until we were waist-deep. Father's silver whistle jolted us, and we dropped into our berths of cobalt water.

I reached the outcrop, jubilant as I touched its rough white curl, and saw at the same instant Paul's dark head a few lengths behind, his arms like brown varnished oars dipping in and out of the sea. Greedy for a win, for the silver dollar, I turned and swam, hardly breathing, until my feet and hands bumped soft sand and I stood, arms raised in what I had practiced earlier in my room as a victory pose. My leg brace lay almost directly in front of me on the beach, but Father was not to be seen. I turned, arms triumphantly upraised, gulping in air. Father, soaked to the neck, had Paul cradled in his arms and was trying to run, slowed by his waterlogged clothes.

In later years, as I struggled within even marginal circumstances, always aware of disappointing my parents, I began to wonder, in those moments when I particularly wanted to place blame outside myself, whether Father hadn't fixed that race, hadn't asked or even paid Paul to let me win, to lay muscle, so to speak, on my character. I never had the courage to insult Father with that question. And after what happened, it seemed beside the point.

ALEX   NAVAL HOSPITAL
SAN FRANCISCO   APRIL 1972

We pull metal chairs, Mother and I, up to the bed. Canvas curtains are drawn around as if to maroon our family upon an island. Hospital sounds, like a low, constant tide, flow beneath the hem of these beige-colored curtains.

Mother says something irrelevant or trivial, as if forgetting where she is. This scrambling of perspective will come to represent a significant expression of her grief. My father is in that last, bitterest stage of emphysema, lungs heavy and silted with water, skin cobalt-tinged, his frame like some example of an extinct, once-impressive species, only its exposed bulk of skeleton left to wonder at.

Two months after Paul's death, less than a year before we left Guam, our family went on a health trip to Hong Kong, Japan, China, and the Philippines. In the port of Shanghai, painted Chinese junks drew up alongside our ship, the *Chaumont*, precariously loaded with cages of sulphur-yellow canaries. Like the other Americans on board, Father bought a canary. It was permitted to fly at liberty throughout the house. It shared my plate at mealtimes, even drinking from my water glass. Once it had been taken off the boat in Shanghai, it never sang again, and lost most of its yellow brilliance. Watery-pale and mute, the canary was my father's apology, his attempt to resurrect a self he had with sad, unintended result altered.

We wait in our canvas island, the three of us. My mother wonders if Maude Hawkins is having bridge luncheon at her house Thursday (Maude Hawkins of course long dead). My father's chest opens and collapses with the hideous wheezing fatigue of an accordion, its pleats cracked, leaking air. It is hot. Reminiscent of the tropics.

Mother pushes vaguely at the curtains, finds her way into the overlit theater of medicine where her husband made his distinguished career, to make a phone call to Maude to ask if her black jersey or blue silk would do better. Perhaps it is as she digs change out from her purse that the hospital monitor begins its shriek, responding to an alteration of heartbeat, that shriek having the same eerie pitch of a particular silver whistle.

A Model T named Blackbird shimmies, veering along paths of rolled, dirty-white coral. Conducted with happy vigor by Clarence Grimmen (a man with a reputation for stern and thorough abilities), two boys hang out the windows, all three off-key and singing to beat the band:

Oh the monkeys have no tails,
They were bitten off by snails . . .
Oh the monkeys have no tails in
Zamboango

I raise my head from the final exhaustion of my father's chest, seeing his face, at last, like Paul's. The dark, dead center between wings.

Rocking on Water,
Floating in Glass

*Never, under any circumstances, allow both your hands to drop to your sides,
unless you want deliberately to display despondency.*

—SARAH BERNHARDT

I would open up the shop, fill the bathroom sink, and write my
name across its flat water. Helen. Helen means light, actually.

Or I would take up the round silver mirror from the vanity set,
carry my face around the unlit adobe rooms, let beveled angles of
light skid across that too-plain face, one eye a yowl of ferocity, the
other pretending, quite convincingly, to be anguished.

I moved about this unfrequented antique shop five days a week.
A displaced person, valueless to collectors, I had tucked up in a
jumble of European antiquities, none of which was dusty because
I proved, for a time, responsible enough to take a soft yellow
cloth to each one. My solitariness was so complete that if the
telephone rang and it was the owner, Clarence, asking how things
were doing, I would feel violated, irritable, interrupted. Rare
times I heard car tires crawling against the gravel, doors slam-

ming, voices with that acquisitive edge, I kept to the shadowy back of the shop, kept an eye that nothing was stolen while whoever they might be circled the rooms, coping with their error in stopping. People driving through New Mexico do not want Oriental rugs or German china or Venetian glass or black beaded bags or bisque-headed dolls. They want to fall across a bargain on Navajo rugs or old hishi or black Pueblo pottery. So they extricate themselves, backing out as soon as they decently can, uncomfortable that their instincts proved so dull.

When the schools dismissed in the afternoons, I'd be alert for the Spanish girls coming in, bumping down the narrow aisles of the shop like slow, brown scavenger fish, except that their fingertips swept across the jewelry, airy as moths. The objects in the shop made them feel their poverty, their lack. Softly they might ask about some pair of earrings that a collection of their fathers' wallets could not buy. The expensive curiosities were a kind of oblique reproach to them. Their moodiness hung about in the shop even after they'd gone.

Clarence once drove his black truck into Mexico, hauling back a load of painted pots shaped like starved bellies and red clay pots fashioned like frogs and pigs. Some cheap baskets. He piled them carelessly on boards in front of the shop, and in a few days had sold every one. He did this to pay rent on the rooms that held his antiques.

* * *

I found the pornography before I found the dress. Venery of an extreme type, inguinous, immodest torsos, limbs locked in rank puzzles. I kept the magazine hidden beneath the desk blotter after finding it on a shelf in the bathroom closet. The presence of that magazine was bewildering to me because Clarence was not a blatantly sexual man. He certainly showed no interest in me, and we were often alone. He and a male friend had once agreed, after much staring at my face, that I would improve as I grew older. What did they mean? It would not have been out of a certain

triteness of character assessment to guess at Clarence as a homo-
sexual. Yet this magazine, its males with prodigious, botanical-like
penises, its women with neck-stems tipped back or to the side,
their mouths like a trampling of slurred poppies, and thighs
propped in grotesque architectures, this magazine was unques-
tionably intended as a heterosexual stimulant.

The eroticism of the pictures receded, leaving a wash of bla-
tantness, commonness, monotony of theme. I began to spot the
bodily flaws, to be frustrated by the secretive, one-dimensional
faces. I noticed stained wallpaper, the office calendar. Things of
that sort.

The dress I discovered later.

In Clarence's desk I found the key that opened the locked mahogany wardrobe. A skinny serpent of a dress, red and dark as
hemorrhage, smelling of stale powder. Sarah Bernhardt's dress.
Inside this clay house in a half-empty desert, a dress Sarah
Bernhardt had worn. Unpriced, not for sale, Clarence's handwriting on the tag pinned to one sleeve. I drew the dress out from the
ferment of the closet. I took off my own dull skirt and brown
sweater.

* * *

Have I forgotten Louis? The pornography could well have
been his, belonged to him. Louis and I were geographically opposed climates, antipodes. Louis of the bantam but egoistic stat-
ure, pompous in heeled shoes, turtleneck jerseys, and shell neck-
laces; he was one of the first men I knew to wear Danish clogs.
What I hated was his compulsive preening over the number of
elegant women he'd left in New York. Now he hoped to make a
living (a killing is what he actually called it) buying jewelry off the
reservations and reselling it at exaggerated prices in New York and
Los Angeles. I found reason and unreason enough to shudder
whenever he came into the shop. Those high shoes and that sleek,
ferret face, always scenting out profit, advantage. For Louis, I was
not only inexquisite, I was not even there. But then we were civil,

somehow managing to drape a neat shroud over our distaste for one another.

There isn't a thing left to say about him except that he was grateful when I took over his job of sitting in the shop, and that some weeks later Clarence received a phone message that Louis was dead. He had stopped to pick up a fourteen-year-old girl hitchhiking on the Los Angeles freeway. In the car she'd knifed him. His locked briefcase of Indian jewelry was found beside him.

Louis. Pretentious aesthete, cultural parasite, male snob, unbearable egoist. Stabbed by a young girl. Should I hope that at least, in the final moments, she proved exquisite, this child who took his life? The whole irony was excessive and horrible.

A few days afterward, alone in the shop, I went into the kitchen to boil an egg for my lunch, and there was a frog sitting on the dirty white linoleum. A mud-colored heap of a frog. I knew it was Louis. His spirit. I squatted down therefore and spoke to him.

My God, Louis, I am sorry.
I apologize because I never liked you.
There was a certain justice in the way you died,
you know that, don't you?
But, still.

The frog stared at me. What did I think it would do? I put a saucer of water down for it. What did frogs eat or lap at? Hardly like stray cats or dogs. I propped open the back door to let it go. When I left the kitchen, it still hadn't moved. When I came back from the woman who had bought a piece of yellow and white glass, it, or Louis, was gone. There was a small damp spot on the linoleum.

Where his life had merely aggravated me, Louis's manner of death invaded me. That appalling contrast between his attempts at high living, to keep the little finger on high, as it were, and the messy hack-up of his death, in a rented car on the freeway, haunted me badly. There is a theory that people only change under terms of crisis. But the crisis must be surmountable. You must be left alive at the end of it.

To distract myself from what were becoming gruesome musings, I borrowed Clarence's biography of Sarah Bernhardt. I tallied our unlikenesses. I had been born beneath a canopy of social privilege, coddled to near-spinelessness. She had been illegitimate, unwanted, a nuisance left to the inept care of unpaid help. I had lowered myself into a few tepid, one-sided affairs, and been left anemic if not aphasic at the inevitable end of them; she gathered up strength like lilies, mowing down endless pastures of renewable suitors. I kept to the drab corner, the poignant silence, relying on an inner superiority to compensate for the outward plainness; she flaunted herself, blazed above her contemporaries like a force of enormous chemical energy. A planet to herself. Unable to bear solitude. The single trait we shared and in full measure between us was our lack of female beauty.

* * *

Two weeks or so following Louis's knifing, the winter had begun to give way; mild, windy days were drawing up green knobs of hyacinth around the back door. I unlocked the closet in the late afternoon. I had just finished the page on Sarah's deathbed scene. I stood naked in front of her dress.

Before I came here I had mislaid my identity like a glove or small box on the seat of a public bus. I had no bearings left at all. Some people will never know what it is for their lives to go dark and useless. I had found in this shop a place to temporarily absolve myself of human contact. To keep dust off the possessions of the dead was all I had left in me. A mangy, bitten-up jackal, on yellow haunches before the pricey, high gates of extinction. Perhaps I only suffered from some treatable deficiency in the blood. I had turned as colorless as water, as reflective as glass.

Yet even here life had its way of sifting in under the door, seeping its way into the shop of dead forgotten things, extreme and vivid in its inexorable progress . . . murder, pornography, serpents shut away and toads pushing in . . .

The dress fell against my skin as if a multitude of her characters were crowded into it, applauding, hallooing, murmuring, howling, conversing, cajoling. Go on, they said. I heard them plainly. Go on.

Dropping my name, Helen, in the lapping basin. Light rocking on water. Leaving my face floating in the glass. Leaving the phone shrilling.

Walking out onto the highway, straight and pole-upright; under my winter coat, the red, dark, erotic flag, its foreign, gloried standard bearing me up.

Out from these empty places Bernhardt made a promise, extravagant, improbable, and desperately final, to take me.

In Foreign Country

Waiting at the gate of the Costa Rican airport, a frayed palm much like a circus plume splashing upwards from behind his head, Mr. Sykes inadvertently appeared tropical. Pressing around him were shorter, darker-skinned people; her father looked like an endangered white heron rising above a muted carpet of sparrows. Beth pressed Sierra's face to the window of the airplane.

"There's Grandpa, honey, right over there. See the man in the red shorts and blue-checked shirt? Yes he is, he's very tall."

Secured like a flag to its pole, above the heads of the Costa Ricans, his white hair a little napkin of cloud, her father managed to look ridiculous and above question at the same time. He represented benign authority. Monied order. Obedience.

Sloppily, Beth changed Sierra's diaper, wishing there were one last merciful button on her straight skirt to let out. She needed her parents to see how ably she'd coped with divorce. Thin indicated mental health—that was how they were. She blotted orange juice off Sierra's face and rumpled pinafore, her own face glossy with sweat.

"Ok, sweetie, let's go meet Grandpa."

But first Beth pressed her palm to Sierra's forehead. She had been too floppily compliant the last leg of the trip. Her forehead and cheeks burned. Well, Beth felt inhumanly hot. The whole damn plane was hot. Maybe it was a tooth coming in. Would her mother have a baby thermometer? Did they sell baby thermometers here? On her first trip to a foreign country, Beth was already finding things to feel uncertain about.

* * *

The government car was parked in a striped No Parking zone directly in front of the airport's entrance. Mr. Sykes hefted Beth's suitcase into the open trunk. His right leg, withered from childhood polio, held a tremor, the sinews twanging within the damaged instrument of the calf. Above his walnut-tanned legs hung the onion bulb of his middle. Despite these and other assorted departures from the idealized male form, Mr. Sykes impressed people as a dignified and handsome figure.

Sierra's white sandal left a tarry smudge on the back-seat upholstery. A childish terror of punishment resurrected in Beth. She planted Sierra, still oddly placid, squarely over the soiled spot.

"How far to the house, Daddy?"

"Oh, give or take traffic, twenty-five minutes."

They sat at a red light, Beth squinting behind dark glasses, watching women pass in front of the car. Most of them wore designer jeans waxed over rumps jacked to heaven by plastic teetery heels.

"Girls here are dogs, most of them."

"Tight jeans though."

"Listen, that's nothing next to the minis the girls used to wear in Vietnam. What beauties."

Beth couldn't manage a response to her father's nostalgic lust. She resented his classic approach to females, the blatant sexual appraisal overlying blunt contempt. She looked out her window at foreign country.

The equatorial sun was a chemical bath, overexposing the land-

scape, shearing it of detail. Trees were dwarfish. Banana and coffee. Brown-edged palms. Shrubs oily, dark green, with Jello-
bright flowers. More stunted trees. Banana, coffee. More palms.
Houses on the outskirts of San José looked like small, bashed gift
boxes, pink, yellow, blue, slumped pastels. Things held to the
ground by the reverberant snarl of light.

Out of San José, the highway abruptly turned black and fresh.
As her father signaled and slowed to turn left, the car behind them
hit its brakes, averting a near-collision. Mr. Sykes stopped his
government car and got out. The other driver, a well-dressed
Costa Rican man, got out as well. Beth turned to watch out the
back window. Her father, leaning over the much smaller man, his
forefinger pointed into his face, was yelling. *Stúpido. Stúpido.* His
Spanish was terrible. The man's plump decent face appeared
frightened. He bowed and bowed, apologizing. Her father, re-
jecting apology, got back into his car. The other driver got into his
car. Traffic had stopped around them. As Beth turned back in her
seat, she saw the slum out her right window. Roofs made of corrugated tin and walls of packing crates. All doorless. Dust. A few
chickens. Children with large bellies and little clothing, listless,
thumbs in mouths. Dust. She felt trapped and exposed in the
private government car.

"Idiots." Her father slammed the door. "Stupid people. Can't
drive."

They turned into a greener, hilly area, the houses few and pros-
perous looking. Her father followed a curving graded hill with
pearly cement walks, succulent ground covers, sprinkler systems.

"We've had burglaries . . . " He pointed out two blank-eyed
giants of houses, recent victims. "A damned nuisance, of course.
Your mother's worried silly. She had quite a few things stolen,
both in Vietnam and Peru."

Mrs. Sykes had spotted them, was waiting outside the front
door in a parrot-green sleeveless dress and matching sandals. At
sixty she retained the spiked metabolism of a hummingbird. Mrs.
Sykes wrote her daughter in a jittery hum of navy ink, her chatter

most often revolving around the treasonable acts of her aging flesh . . . "I exercise at the club three times a week, but still you should see the flab under my arms, rocking like a hammock. Oh, I wish I could take the scissors and whack it all off. Terrible getting old, Bethey."

Mr. Sykes headed off to make afternoon martinis while Beth was shown the maid, a skewbald woman with the narrowing head and long legs of a greyhound. Mercedes offered Sierra a Pepperidge Farm cookie which she refused, preferring to trail listlessly after her mother and grandmother. Mrs. Sykes adored the notion of a grandchild, but Beth guessed the strain of the actual presence would be telling by dinner.

The Spanish-style house had low ceilings, long narrow corridors, white plaster walls, and floors of oxblood tile. Mrs. Sykes, dickering and plundering her way through a series of impoverished countries, had acquired a great deal. This, then, was an ethnic job lot of a house, a charm bracelet. Rooms dangling with Turkish copper, blue donkey beads, Vietnamese ceramic planters and elephant end tables, Peruvian and Guatemalan wall hangings, molas, ponchos, shreds of cultures picked clean, nailed to walls, strewn across floors. A Bolivian cowboy's stirrups leaned against the black cast-iron head of a Vietnamese peasant girl. Jarring the mood, displaced on a wall outside her parents' bedroom, hung a collection of photographs. Beth's Childhood. Beth's Adolescence. Beth at College. Far too many pictures of Beth and Jared as Parents with Baby Sierra. There were no current pictures, none of Beth Divorced and Unemployed.

When Mrs. Sykes disappeared into her walk-in closet to fetch something for Sierra, Beth followed.

"Ye gods, Mother."

Mrs. Sykes turned. "What, dear?"

Hundreds of clothes were fastidiously hung according to color and function. Hundreds. Under their varied hems lay field rows upon field rows of shoes. Beth counted ten shades of one style of sandal alone. The volume, its meticulous arrangement, was extremely unsettling to Beth. It suggested ungenerous things about her mother.

Sensing criticism, Mrs. Sykes retaliated.

"Have you and Jared attempted any sort of reconciliation?"

"No, we haven't. I doubt we will."

"I cannot understand you young people. So quick to call it quits. He was very good for you, Bethey. Your father and I thought worlds of Jared. In our day we hung on, you know."

"Mother, there's no need to exclude Jared from the present tense. He's absent by choice, not dead."

"And poor baby . . ." Mrs. Sykes referred to Sierra, wriggling her pink blocklike feet greedily into the toe-ends of each of Grandma's shoes, showing animation at last. "Oh, honey, not those, sweetie, careful, those are Grandma's best, when does she get a chance to be with her daddy? It can't be healthy for a little girl to grow up without her daddy."

"She sees him twice a month. More if he wants."

Beth walked out, hoping to find her father and his martinis.

* * *

Beth's mother fussed, packing up two native-woven baskets, laying beach towels over the car seats. Beth lapsed into the impotency of childhood, standing and waiting for Mother, holding the hats, towels, extra shoes, lotions, changes of clothing. In their family, any expedition was burdened by anticipation of calamity. Everyone got worked into frayed irritability by all the cautious detail. Thus they had rarely gone anywhere, and not until Beth was in college did her father join the State Department. Even now, Mr. Sykes preferred to stay home with his granddaughter, who, as it turned out, was teething and running a slight temperature. They'd eat lunch, take their naps together, Mr. Sykes predicted cheerily.

So her mother drove, hands sliding and slapping around the steering wheel, rings tapping, a nervous hub of energy. Beth experienced a sort of reactive apathy around her mother, her neck would stiffen, she would get quiet and heavy-bodied, narcoleptic. Mrs. Sykes, driving by an unstable collection of tin and crate shacks piled into a hillside, voiced one of her emphatically subjective opinions.

"What you should realize is that these people don't attempt to better themselves. I'm not saying anyone likes to live that way, but we've tried. Oh, have we tried. Brought in health and sanitation experts, educators, birth control people. In any country you have the smart ones who take the ball, and then you have the rest. What do you do with them? The press certainly has a field day. And something else, Bethey. These people aren't so poor or put upon as the press would have you believe back home. No-o. I know for a fact Mercedes has money squirreled away. Most of them do."

Beth's head ached.

The country club had the same vegetation Beth had seen all over Costa Rica, but here it was landscaped and looked expensive. The parking lot was full of new, imported cars. Standing by the car, holding all the junk her mother was handing her, Beth noticed the men staring at her. Two men raking leaves out of a bed of flowering shrubs had stopped, rakes lifted, to stare. She felt a slight hiccup of foolishness standing there with folk baskets, in a handmade tunic top, wearing a straw hat. One of the gardeners wore a hat like hers, but without any ribbon. Beth remembered the anti-American graffiti sprayed in curling red across concrete walls inside San José.

Mrs. Sykes, oblivious and smelling of frangipani, flip-flopped in her sandals into the club and signed them in. The air was deodorized, artificially cooled, and thinly scored with Muzak. Beth sat on a piece of expensive country club furniture. Everywhere was the unsubtle smack of privilege.

"Oh look," said Mrs. Sykes, "there goes Ricardo. The club's masseur. Ricardo. Oh Ricard-oh."

The masseur was a muscular, middle-aged man who looked alternately cynical and obsequious.

"I'd like you to meet my daughter, Elizabeth. Ricardo gives me my massage twice a week. I could not live without a minute of it. I'm spoiled, and don't we know it?"

Ricardo laughed with the appropriate measure of muzzy embarrassment. His hands hung from his wrists like malleted club steaks.

"Nice to meet you," Beth murmured.

They carried their baskets into a curtained cubicle. Beth changed rapidly, her back to her mother, humiliated by her stomach, still quaggy from childbirth, her navel like a clogged button in the white, pouchy ottoman of her belly. Her turquoise suit cut like a pastry wheel into her thighs. Her mother, ever impatient with modesty, stood slapping and slewing lotion on her arms and legs, her nude body a freckly red-brown. Mother, plunging viciously through the dress racks in stores, kneading Beth's scalp with her bony knuckles whenever she shampooed her hair. Noisy with peasant blood, Mother used to say. Can't help it. Can't keep still. Irish blood, wasn't it? Beth's body was beginning to mimic her mother's, the loose stomach, breasts like narrow tubular bells. All those vain attempts to bar her mother from department-store dressing rooms. "Hell's bells, Elizabeth Sykes! Who's changed your diapers? I've seen you all your life!" All the same, Beth would feel her mother's stare on her, excoriating, greedy.

They went out by the pool, laid towels over chaise longues. Where were the owners of the shiny cars in the parking lot? The pool area was nearly deserted. Two mothers with bonneted toddlers sat on the sloped wet edge of the wading pool. They wore bikinis and spoke exuberant French.

"Wouldn't Sierra love that wading pool, Bethey? We must bring her along next time."

The sun was a goliath opponent. Beth felt her skin crack in its overwhite glaze, the sunblock she'd put on a joke.

Mrs. Sykes descended the pool steps. She swam as Beth remembered her mother swimming, a clumsy backstroke, hands groping backwards, clutching the skin of water, her face clenched, as if to relax would insure a deadfall to the bottom. Beth swam on her stomach, her face in the water, the brunt of sun on her back. She swam until her muscles hurt.

"I've got to get under an umbrella, Mother." Her mother's chest and arms and legs sparkled like broiled poultry. Her straw hat hid her face. Beth remembered an energetic mother in shirt-waist dresses, scrubbing floors on her hands and knees, sponging down walls, raging over dust compressed and gray and dry inside venetian blinds. Now having some close-of-life, slightly forced fling at privileged life. The bittersweet complaints about lazy maids, her amusing golf caddy, irreplaceable masseur. People who stood about, paid to wait on her mother's surface needs.

✳ ✳ ✳

It was a relief to get up from the table where her father ate in afflicted silence, elbows spraddling the table, eyes focused on an overladen plate, this habit of eating flogged on by deeper, unseen unsatisfied appetites. It was a relief to exit a house where Mercedes redundantly swiped over perfectly polished surfaces while Mrs. Sykes stood by, stage-whispering to Beth, "She knows whatever we've got, you realize."

Yet Beth found herself unmoved, felt a lack of resonance as they drove, as she looked at foreign country out the windows of the car. They were headed for a village frequented by tourists during Easter week festivities. They arrived late, just as the pageant had ended. Young men slouched against stucco walls, costumed in the scarlet and gold livery of ancient Roman soldiers. Many of them were drinking from green glass bottles of Coke. Mrs. Sykes jabbed her finger out the open window.

"Look, Bethey, there. The crucifixion."

In the central plaza of the village rose a modest hill. An iron-work grille separated it from ordinary events. At its little summit stood three wooden crosses; at the base of each posed a figure, in striped livery, with plumed helmet and halberd.

"My God," Beth said, "no one's actually nailed up there?" She was thinking of the town criminals and insane.

"Oh heavens no, those figures are cloth. On Good Friday the village will turn out to act various parts in the Passion. We heard from the Winchells, who went last year, remember that, Daddy? It's supposed to be fascinating."

The narrow streets were unpaved and lined with low stucco apartments in blistered pinks, watery blues and greens. Teenaged boys in American jeans swarmed over the sidewalks around the plaza, playing transistor radios, roller-skating, wearing dark glasses.

Grasping Sierra's hand, Beth ascended shallow steps toward the stone church brooding with high, rose-gray walls over the spotty village with its chancres of Westernization, faded red Coke machines and movie posters, its boys like one great mobile longing for the fabled excesses of youth in America.

Within the plain interior of the church were the old people. Beth stood in a back corner. A man and woman stepped into the church, the sun a squared yellow palm heeling them in. The woman had knotted a black scarf over her head, the man wore baggy trousers and an orange shirt. They crossed themselves with holy water and knelt down. Beth heard the stiff crack of their bones. Heads bowed, they began to shuffle, on their knees, across an uneven stone floor. Toward the altar.

Beth had never fallen to her knees. For no one, for no belief, had she or anyone she knew publicly humbled themselves. While her mother took Sierra out to find a soft drink, Beth stayed, reluctant to leave a sight so foreign, so moving to her.

✳ ✳ ✳

When they got home, Mrs. Sykes had two domestic crises to cope with. She came out of the kitchen puffed and heated-looking.

"Oh, just look at what the dumdum did now. She put the wrong polish on my Turkish ashtrays. Just look at them." The copper-rimmed enamel dishes were a solid gray-green. "And she put wax down on the kitchen floor after I've told and told her not to do that. Damn."

"Mother, calm down. The poor woman doesn't have your sophisticated knowledge of cleaning products. She can't read English directions. And this place is already so immaculate she can't possibly imagine what it is she's supposed to be cleaning. So she invents something like ruining your Turkish ashtrays. She's practically unnecessary, except perhaps for your laundry. Though, of course she must need whatever money you pay her."

Mrs. Sykes calmed, but insisted there was a great deal of housework. The maids were just dumdums and they were always getting pregnant. Oh, everyone complained about them. She'd never find anyone to match Phong. Phong kept things trim as a pin, made lemon meringue pie from scratch, gave Dad his backrubs, and was jolly besides. Beth had read her mother's letters from Saigon, praising someone named Phong, now vanished in the fabric of a new regime.

"Maybe you should have smuggled her out."

Beth was being facetious, picturing a jolly Chinese woman crated up along with all her mother's other possessions.

But Mrs. Sykes was feeling cheated out of excellent help by a civil war. "I wish I had," she said darkly.

* * *

Beth and Sierra were now driven every day to the country club. Sierra splashed and dabbled in the wading pool just as she did in her plastic pool at home. Beth followed her mother in and out of the more expensive gift shops in San José, toured the National Museum with its pre-Columbian exhibits, clay frogs and gold lizards, jaguar-headed grinding stones, and grimacing nudes with square mouths and splayed thighs. Twice she ate lunch in a French restaurant while reading in English newspapers about a recent bomb scare in the American embassy and a kidnapped American oil executive whose body was found decomposed by a roadside. Anti-American graffiti was not being washed off the city's walls, and angry, unsigned letters were being sent in about it.

Beth went to see her father in his eighth-floor air-conditioned office. She met his secretaries, who were gregarious and bright and amused Sierra by letting her punch away at an old typewriter.

Her father's office looked achingly bare, his chair swiveled to face the street as though he only sat there, looking down at people. His desk was uncluttered, without the air of busy authority she remembered from his other offices.

On the day before she and Sierra were to fly home (Beth would have to begin looking for a job as well as good day care), her father caught his commuter bus into the city while her mother walked down the block to attend her monthly bridge luncheon. Beth, Sierra, and the maid were left alone for the afternoon.

In the boxlike laundry room off the kitchen, Mercedes scrubbed at a stain in one of Beth's blouses, using a small orange hand-brush. Beth stood at the deep cement sink, wishing to communicate good faith and a sense of equality, wishing to separate herself from her parents. Mercedes was polite, clearly unresponsive, so Beth, watching the mound of her own dirty clothes being fed by the maid into the soapy water, backed out of the damp little room.

She spooned a banana yogurt into Sierra, read her a story-book, kissed her, and put her down for a nap. She began restlessly to walk around her parents' house. Everything was paired, seam-less, in sterile conjunction. Yet beneath that rigid cloth of ap-pearance were swept such messy, ancient, unfixable moments. An oppressive sterility framed her mother's bargained-for things. Space scoured of life's complications, crammed with its hand-made evidence. Things which could be tidied up, made accept-able, unlike the people who made and sold these things to feed their families.

Beth saw her mother's car keys on the hall table, attached like a jailer's to a heavy brass hoop. If she refused to be encumbered by any idea of crisis, she could leave.

She went back into the wet-smelling laundry room where Mer-cedes was now ironing Beth's nightgown, and in hobbled Span-ish explained that she would return in two hours, that the baby was asleep and Mrs. Sykes would be home by three. Mercedes, she knew, stayed every day until four-thirty.

The ease of her escape excited her. When she got to San José,

Beth parked half a block from the enormous, green-roofed open market her mother had hurried her past a few days before. She threw some flirtatious swing into her walk; there was new, exotic visibility in being here alone.

In the noisy market Beth wandered down aisles, passing souvenir T-shirts, feathered toys, leather purses, sandals. Dark syrupy stains mapped the concrete flooring. The flies were turgid, sloppy-crawling, unpursued and unhurried. Flaring pink, sulphurous yellow, madonna blue, the dyed sweets and candies, the ices scooped into paper cones. A cat slunk against Beth's bare calves, each of its ribs vaulted and isolate. Plumy black tail quivering, a dog urinated against the corner of a booth. The place stunned and drugged the senses like the flabby, stinking blossom of a carniverous plant. Camera around her neck, straw purse over one shoulder, Beth stopped with an almost voyeurish morbidity when she came to the meat and fish stands. Lines of women stood with baskets, buying for dinner. Quarries of meat slow-waltzed from the arms of black metal hooks, flies sparkled like moving sequins over the marbled flesh. Whole chickens lay unplucked, necks wrung, in stupid, open-eyed assemblage. Chicken feet swung on strings, like clawed marionettes. Fish were splayed in half-open fans on gray-brown ice shavings. In all the humid, sweet-rot, heavy air nothing was kept in plastic wrapping, nothing protected.

Beth had now come to an empty area, a square block section of empty booths with stale, lingering smells. Over against a corrugated metal wall two men squatted, passing a cigarette between them. They were old, and Beth crept towards them, her camera flash ready. But they saw her and one of the men jabbed out his tongue, rolled it noisily in and out at her, in soft sucking circles. The other man wrinkled his eyes in passive, monkeylike mirth. Beth swerved, walking rapidly down the deserted aisles. It was eerily silent and far from the market. She smelled marijuana smoke at the same time as five or six teenaged boys came shoving one another out of a public urinal. Seeing Beth, they stopped.

She thought first, crazily, of her camera. Then her gold necklace. Her good watch. Her body. Her sex. Sounds of the market were far and faint. No one knew where she was. Some balance had tipped against her.

Beth ran down blind aisles, her camera knocking painfully at her chest. Ran for the noise and safety of the market. Ran past the old men she had attempted to photograph; this time they looked right through her.

As her panic abated, she decided she had been foolish. She passed iridescent meats, the hills of vegetables, the woven baskets, jowled hammocks, cheap imported radios.

Face and chest flushed, hair sweaty against her neck, Beth feigned shopping, touching things while getting her breath back. It calmed, to run her hands over things for sale. She felt safe. When the children approached her, she was able to smile down at them. Three girls, each waving a sheet of local newspaper. Did senora want to buy? No, no, Beth shook her head, no. Thank you, no. They were pushing so affectionately against her, blowing kisses, so oddly persistent. Until she felt a tug at her watch. A slight pulling at her purse. She snared the hard, bony wrist of the older girl.

"Give it to me. My wallet. My money."

The girls shook their heads, no, senora, no, *inocente,* no money. They pulled their ragged dresses over their heads, the oldest girl ripping open her thin blouse so her tiny purple nipples jutted up on scarcely formed breasts. Their underwear was gray and torn, their bodies skinny, hard. People stopped, gathered, watched. Beth felt vicious anger warping the space in her chest.

"Give me my wallet, my money, or I will call the police. *Policía! Policía!*" she screamed, keeping her grip now on two of the girls. The older girl sighed, defeated, and held out the wallet. Beth grabbed it. The children backed into the crowd and no one stopped them.

Oh, but her watch. It was gone. The people stood, staring at her, saying nothing, their faces carefully washed of expression.

What, did they think she should have given those little thieves her money? They are children, the eyes said. Their families maybe live on the streets, the faces said. But I'm not rich and it isn't right to steal, is it? She wanted to scream, "Leave me alone, I haven't much more than you."

Beth found her father's government car and climbed into its clean refuge, its safe order. She locked each of the doors, rolled up the windows, turned on the air conditioner, put on her dark glasses.

* * *

The house was unchanged, cool, hushed. Mercedes sat at the kitchen table, eyeing a soap opera, muttering advice to one of the characters.

Beth went down the long corridor and found Sierra standing in the crib, sweaty curls stuck to her head, sobbing, hiccuping. The maid had let her cry like this? Surely she could have heard her. If the television weren't on. If she'd bothered to check. Beth wondered at the depth of hostility that might lie behind the woman's impassive politeness.

* * *

That last night, Beth sat with her father on the tiny cement patio while her mother gave Sierra a bath. Mr. Sykes sat in the shadow of his house, the smell of gin and hibiscus around him, talking about what he would do if he were really wealthy. It had something to do with a yacht, with traveling. He did not mention Beth's mother.

As he got up heavily to get another drink, Beth thought about telling him what had happened to her in the market. She heard him limp, with his weakened leg, into the dining room and say, "Well, that's life," either to himself or to her, it didn't seem clear, but in such an enormously passive and resigned way that Beth was made to understand that her father had turned old. Telling him would confirm his opinion of her sloppy naiveté, the soundness of his own prejudice. He would use what had happened to prove himself right.

* * *

On the small Costa Rican airplane she and Sierra were given seats beside a European-looking man with cropped red hair and a vigorous profile. Her parents were out there, still standing by the gate. White-haired, tanned, in pressed expensive clothing. It was the fact of commitment kept, no matter what, her mother believed, that meant something in the end. People drifted past them like strings of dark kelp. Her parents looked frail as exotic wreckage from a ship. Beth was almost afraid for them, afraid to leave them.

"I don't have a watch," she told the man, who had put down his plastic folding table and begun to work on a long series of mathematical equations.

"I lost my watch," she amended, sparing herself the humiliation of any whole truth. "Can you tell me what time it is?"

Sierra sucked at a bottle. The plane lurched as it rose, the mountains looked hideously lush, and Beth was terrified of how close she was to those mountains. She could see individual trees. Ebony, mahogany, balsa, her father had said. The plane wasn't ascending, wasn't it drifting, in fact, sinking?

She touched the European man's arm. "Is this normal? Should the plane be doing this?" What she meant was, are my daughter and I going to die now, in this accidental way?

"Oh, no. I've flown these planes many times. It's always like this. You'll see." He went immediately back to his work.

The plane did rise, did take true course. Beth looked at the pale green grid paper the man was using. He penciled numbers into squares; eventually, he would arrive at unarguable answers.

There is nothing, she wanted to say to this man, orderly, or capable of staying in place, uncompromised. You distract yourself. You pay a price for this abstract perfection.

Sierra had climbed off her seat and gone down the aisle, making Beth glad of an excuse to leave this man with his illusionary sense of safety. She gathered up their things and followed. Locating a row of vacant seats, she settled her daughter in, then looked out the window as they rose high over the foreign place—with its row upon row of unworn shoes, its men submissive to accident, its children, indicted for what?

Holding Sierra's hand for comfort, Beth continued to look out the window of the plane, drawing back only when the equatorial sun invaded, striking her with its flat, reflected glare.

Photograph of Luisa

Since there are no phone booths in a ghost town, I wrote a postcard. The postcard was white, which bothered me, so I colored it. On top of the red smear, with a black crayon, I printed:

DEAR RATTLESNAKE KILLER,
    PLEASE COME RIGHT AWAY.
        LUISA
p.s. we have money this time

It was two weeks or more before he came and he wasn't even the same man as before. Maybe he was his son, that's what I thought at the time. But before you hear about that, I want to tell you about Luisa.

Luisa's hair pushes out from the underside of her skull, then splits into two branches, or better yet, black forks. Her mouth, it is wide, her fingers tell me that it is wide. She is blind so she must not use her fingers. Poor blind Luisa. I'm fooling you, hah, I'm not blind. But sometimes I would like to turn in the direction of my mother and be prevented from seeing her. My mother, who is quite old, sits in a chair on the porch, near the railing. She whispers that because of me she breathes in red dust all day. Since the photographs came, I have neglected her. I have stopped wondering if she will punish me forever. Carelessly now, I tend my mother. She is too choked up with that dust to thank me.

We live in this ghost town which is a very phony ghost town. It is an old movie set where Henry Fonda used to make westerns. Mr. Sanchez, whose head is yellow-empty like a dried gourd, sighs. "Maybe they'll come back some day and make another movie." And then he shakes his head at me. "Maybe they'll have a part in the movie for you, Luisa." He is quite serious. Hah, I say to him. Hah.

I wrote the rattlesnake killer because they are all over the place this summer. I see and hear one every day. My mother is not especially worried; she boasts that they have many times hiked up her legs to warm themselves in her stone of a lap. Mr. Sanchez even left me a shotgun, but I don't remember how to use it. Have you ever held a rifle every which way and then put it away for good?

In the mornings I'm up in the dark, up when it's still cool. I shake out my hair and go tend the animals, pouring water for them. I don't wear clothes then, I don't wear boots. I am careful not to step on anything living. To step on a living thing, to harm a life, is to have that life and maybe other lives follow you around to the end of your days, that's what my mother believes.

And when it's still so dark and I am with the animals, I can watch my reflection pouring out in the hard dark water. It is the time when ghosts matter least.

After swinging shut the corral gate, I climb up on the rail and face the peak, the Cabezon, watching for the sun which jumps up from behind it. A spit of river circles the base of the mesa, and it's all the water we have here, for the animals, for my mother who thirsts, for the tourists who come. Mr. Sanchez calls them tourists so I do too, because that is my job. When they drive up here lost, I quietly tell them that this is a ghost town and for fifty cents, even though I am blind, I can give them a pretty good tour. And they're hot and tired and curious because a minute ago they were lost and bad tempered, and now they're in a ghost town with a girl with hair split in two and eyes that see everything.

To fence up a desert is to make a dry pasture. Fencing is almost all there is here. Down the road is an abandoned house, red adobe, tin roof, no glass in the windows, no door in the doorway, and an old white washer tipped against one wall. Mr. Sanchez keeps a herd of spotted horses near here. That's all there is, that's it, besides a certain ghost town which, before the sunlight has a chance at it, is cold and blue.

I gulp coffee, spitting out the grounds, and watch my town lose its blue coldness. When the sun is up, the wood buildings are bleached and warped loose; the street, rutted red clay. (I have wiped such reddish stuff off my brother's face and fastened it like a mask, with guilty fingers, over my own. In dreams, my mother saw death approach our house through a different door. Over and over, in her dreams, death had both of us.)

I must go inside and dress before my mother wakes up.

Each day I have expected him. Each day nothing. This morning I wake up and go outside, and I know when my feet hit the ground that someone is approaching the ghost town. I hear no car on the road, but I can feel the clay shaking gently beneath me. I water the animals—the chickens, the goats, and the donkey—then I go back and get dressed right away and sit out on the steps, waiting. I wait for hours, until the blue wood is bleached and warped loose and I hear my mother's bare feet whispering behind me on the porch.

He does not come as a speck of horizon getting larger and larger. He is quietly there, at the end of the street, on his horse. As I said in the beginning, I am surprised because he is not the one I remember from last time. Maybe, I think, this is his son. He leans down to me over his sweating horse. He sweats too. He is fat, very loose around the belly. He wears a holy medallion around his neck and a dirty leather vest. A black cowboy hat with a short dyed feather shades his face. There is a bag for collecting the snakes in. I see his belt is made of the snakeskin.

He says something, and I point to all the places where I have seen them lately. I turn a little and point into one dark house, then another. He nods, slides off his horse and ties it to a weak railing. I go to fetch water. The horse drinks, the man drinks. Loosely holding his rifle, he hooks the sack to his belt, nods at me again, and heads around the back of the street. He has much work to do, so I creep up the steps and sit by my mother. I rest my head on her knee and her hand smooths my hair. The first shot is fired. Her hand stops forever, then continues.

Later he sits on the steps, rubbing his forehead with a red cloth. Even when there is no dampness left, he keeps wiping, slowly, across his forehead. His horse stands in a finger of shade, flies marching around its eyes and muzzle. I am standing here in the doorway of my house and I think of looking for the sack. It is slumped in clay by the feet of the man. It is not even half full. Maybe he is not finished. Maybe he is not so good a shot as the other man. Maybe he doesn't guess where they hide by day as well as I do.

He looks into the wetness on the red cloth and says, "Weren't as many as I'd expected to find." Now he is turned, looking at me through his square dark glasses. He keeps watching me. I am breaking off bits of wood from the doorway with my fingers. I am not used to people. I am not accustomed to anything living. His watching, his not saying anything while he watches, reminds me of that.

He asks my name.

"Luisa Jaramillo."

"Luisa, I'd like to ask you a favor."

"Sure," I say, meaning no. You can have water, that's all. "Sure,"
I say.

He pauses, looks over at his horse. "I'm a photographer, Luisa,
not a snake killer. An amateur snake killer, a professional photographer. I am also a tourist, not from here."

My fingers peel off a sliver of wood that catches and jabs under
my nail. Even my mother is quiet but awake.

"I asked the old man who usually comes out here to help you if
I could do the job for him. You see, he's been sick since this past
winter and I thought I'd help him out and me at the same time."
He points to the sack. "Rotten work."

I am looking at him fearfully, wondering if he got them all.

"When he told me about this ghost town and about you living
out here, taking care of this place . . ."

The place takes care of itself. I take care of my mother and water
the animals.

". . . I got interested. Maybe some great pictures, I thought.
Anyway, Luisa . . ." Now he's looking at me, he has taken off his
glasses and his eyes are light gray, ghost rock. He knows nothing
about me.

"I would like to ask your permission to shoot some pictures."

"Of what?" I ask. My voice comes from the sliver of wood
under my nail, slight but painful.

"Of you, in this town."

"There are only ghosts here," I insist in a quiet voice.

"Well yes, it must seem so by now." He sounds surprised but
not curious.

"Will you let me, Luisa?"

I answer him.

He gets to his feet as if he has already forgotten me and goes to
his horse, to the saddlebag. I come out to the steps, following him
that far.

"I've never had my picture taken," I say loudly. He is not far off,
but his back is to me, so I yell.

"It won't hurt," he hollers back. He is getting out some kind of camera equipment; he brings it back to the porch and sits on the steps, working with it.

"What's your name?" I ask.

He looks at me. "I'll be ready for you in a minute."

I look away and wait.

By sunset he is finished. I am glad at first, but after he gets up from the steps where we have sat together and goes over to his horse, I feel the connection of film between us breaking. His camera, full of me and my mother, is in the saddlebag.

He lifts the sack and ties it to the saddle. I can see curves through the burlap sacking, long cold coils. I am certain he didn't get them all. I feel very unsafe, very frightened, unable to speak.

He is on his horse, which I imagine is white, then brown grows over many parts of what I have imagined, and he is on his spotted horse, leaning down to me. His hand reaches out and smooths my hair the way my mother's did while he was killing those snakes with his gun.

"The old man tells me that people have grown afraid for you."

I am looking at the horse's red-rimmed hooves, at the tail switching drily between the two back legs. I want this man to know that ghost town pictures will disappoint him.

"Luisa, it was not your fault, what happened. You are no longer blamed." He runs his hand down my face, around my eyes.

"You cannot bury yourself here."

I am sure it is wind or dream and not a human gesture.

I sit on the railing of the corral; the donkey nudges her dry nose against my leg. I am facing Cabezon, the large head, I told him, that's what it means. Large head. He took a picture of me standing in front of it.

I am here for a long time. The light that is left is so brief. There is no moon to cover the stars. The points of the stars which can pierce holes in my skin are beauty. Cabezon is beauty.

"It was not your fault . . . the people have grown afraid for you . . ."

I am among ghosts, where I belong.

Mr. Sanchez's pickup is coming up the road from town. I stop sweeping to watch. Red dust already blows back onto the porch and into the house, but I like the temporary cleanness. His truck stops a few feet from me. I drop the broom and run down to look inside the bags in the back of the pickup. The truck is bright blue. I'd like to tease Mr. Sanchez that he is trying to be an Indian driving around in his turquoise truck. That's what they all buy, those Indians, that color of truck.

"Well here you are, Luisa." He is helping carry the paper sacks into the house, into the kitchen, which is in back. He is listing off everything he bought, his old man's voice like dried seeds inside his throat, rattling. "Bread, cheese, meat, tortillas, chillies, pastries, coffee," and then he rummages around in one smaller bag until he brings it out and waves the small package cheerfully.

"Ballpoint pens, this time, Luisa, no crayons. You're too old for those crayons. Yah, you are, so I brought you some ballpointed pens and maybe now you can write some of your family, Luisa. They miss you, you know." And to hide his embarrassment or whatever, he reaches into another bag sitting on the sink and "Here," he waves this around too, "a box of real stationery." He is so pleased by his gifts that I almost smile too.

He remembers something. "Mail, Luisa. You got a package in the mail."

As he goes out of the kitchen I put away the cans and bottles and jars and noisy plastic packages. I have set aside the ballpoint pens and the box of stationery. Oh, this has happened before. He has tried this change before. I hear the truck door open and slam shut. I stand still and look around at the kitchen wall, thickly blotted with squares of paper. Every space of wall has a crayon drawing taped to it. One wall is for my mother's slow, careful drawings; the rest of it is all for me. We color in the evenings, sorting through the crayons on the table; my mother makes shapes of guns and boy figures lying flat with red snakes crawling off them onto the black wavy line that means earth to her, then she colors everything she remembers back over with white. Me, I rub one color on top of another. It helps to use red. Many of my papers are colored over with various reds, but I have never found the perfect shade or shape. And Mr. Sanchez brings us ballpoint pens and stationery.

I look at this old man with suspicion as he hands me a thick brown envelope. He leaves me alone with it. Perhaps he understands that if you never receive mail from anybody, a large brown envelope with your name all over it should not be fussed over.

He has gone out to the porch to talk with my mother. I never know what they find to talk about or even if she answers him with anything but her monotonous whispers. But Mr. Sanchez is a respectful man.

I go outside, not letting go of my envelope. It feels like a rock through its covering. And on the porch now, he and I talk about the animals, the carrying of water from the river, and the rattlesnakes. I try to say that they are mostly gone, that I have seen only one in all the time since the man left. But all that Mr. Sanchez hears is how frightened I am of them, of how unsafe I feel.

"Hey, it's the end of the summer now," he reassures me. "They'll soon feel sleepy and crawl underground," and he talks about the piñon and the cedar firewood that he has already brought in great bundles down from the mountains.

After he climbs into his truck, I ask about his family, his wife and children, whom I have never met. He quietly answers that they are fine, all fine. Polite, I ask nothing more. I thank him then for the groceries, oh, and for the pens and writing paper too.

"That's ok, Luisa, that's ok." Now it is his turn to say what he says to me each time. "The day you can forgive yourself, Luisa, that day you will come away from here."

A statue of an all-embracing Jesus stands on the dashboard of his truck; rosary beads hang from the mirror.

"It is bad, Luisa, to live like you do, seeing no one."

I wait until I see his speck of turquoise stopped by the pasture down the road. I decide where to sit to open my package. I go out by the corral and sit on the ground in a bit of shade. I face Cabezon. The spotted horses are grazing down by the river, their tails dipping like brushes into the muddy water. My hair falls forward, its two black branches shelter my face.

A Mexican woman sits on a painted chair inside her simple adobe house. Behind her are geranium plants on the windowsill, bursting out of coffee cans. Her hands are folded in her rutted lap. *Families,* this book is called. I open it tenderly, the spine cracks. I turn cool pages, watching photographs go by. I care nothing about these people, these mesas, these ranches outside of town. I see low mud houses, narrow streets, sly faces, wondering faces, but they are uninvited in my memory. I turn pages, or maybe breath from Cabezon, from the large head, helps turn them for me. I see my sister, my pretty little sister; she is crouched against the white stucco wall of our old house. The way her face looks, the way her hands are not childlike but are pressed behind her into the wall, hurts me. The pages are lifted from my fingers by the wind from Cabezon. It is not a large book, nearly finished.

Then I see this one page and lean close to it, rocking back and forth. Mamma's chair is on the ghost porch, near the rail, but it does not hold Mamma in its lap. In this photograph the chair is brimming with air and dust. Oh, I might have told him, ghost town pictures would disappoint him with their nothingness.

Now I am wrong. For here is a photograph of Luisa against the town. Luisa's hair, Luisa's blind eyes, the old clay-spotted shirt of Luisa's.

See, Mamma. I am visible. I am in a photograph. You are not

in a photograph. You stop now, stop whispering behind me. I should be forgiven.

This book disappears into its envelope. Sometime I will look at it again. I had meant to tell that man with the sweating belly that ghost town pictures would show him nothing. Poor blind Luisa, he would have said. For in this book of his, what breathes red dust in Mamma's chair, what will not forgive, is shown as nothing, and what is visible in a clay-spotted blouse is me.

I aimed your rifle foolishly; it gave such a little warning, and, as Mamma knew, dreams are dangerous. Dreams will come after you.

Perhaps the people of the town should not be afraid for Luisa. Perhaps the part of Luisa that exists in photographs and is blameless will walk along the black wavy line that means earth, towards home.

And the part of Luisa which must remain, in Mamma's dream, dead alongside the dead, will open wide her eyes, and with Mr. Sanchez's old rifle frighten those snakes underground, before winter. Hah.

A Dance with Alison

Life goes after you.
Evolved, poker-faced, brimming with wits.
You are twelve. Jowled baby—lengthening limbs.
It picks its time, its place. Lights out after you.
Looks up, grinning, from the feast and bony wrack
of your Innocence.

My parents must have driven me those four hours north. I don't recall. But at that girls' camp in the California Sierras I was eleven and outgoing enough to write, direct, and star in an outdoor theater show. Afterward, I sported the black bowler I'd worn in my performance. A happy eccentricity. By the end, there were so many promises, embraces. I took home everyone's address, made everyone go home with mine.

The second year was more than a failed attempt to repeat success, more than the shadowy onset of puberty. These counted, of course, but I think it was my own reversal from light to dark, from stroking along the shimmering surfaces of lakes to diving below, looking for mossed, gravelike objects, for what was camouflaged, almost erotic debris. I picked things up to look at their undersides. Examined the underbelly of myself, of everything. This was my new preoccupation, and I was broody with it, self-absorbed, pricking up my ears only to the grotesque, the violent bits. Ghost stories were nothing.

One of my bunkmates liked to wear tight lavender shorts, cheap lace halter tops with a pointy bra built in, white shoes with scuffed, snouty heels, and pasty commas of violet eye shadow. (My breasts were swelling a little. I would mash them under my crossed arms one minute, inflate my humpy chest the next, uncertain how I should ever learn to live with them.) The girls avoided Denise, but I hung close, hearing how she shoplifted back home, which boys had taken turns feeling her up, and how great this book was she'd brought with her. I read it, read *I Was a Teen-aged Dope Addict* by flashlight in the blood-bright, felted throat of my sleeping bag. I didn't admire or try to emulate Denise, I shunned her as much as anyone. She was just more dark debris I needed to collect.

After an hour's spree in town, I was crazy about a ring I'd bought. The red camp truck rolled down chutes of rock-pitted roads, us singing "This Land Is Your Land" and "Oh, They Had to Carry Harry to the Ferry." The ring cost three dollars. Beneath its convex oval, tats of iridescent butterfly wing were pieced to suggest Sunset Over Lake Tahoe, black jags of pine in the background. That butterflies had been hunted down for this did not occur to me. I wore the ring much as I had worn the black bowler the year before.

Now what I am coming to, what I am in this HIGH HOLY HEAT to confess, is my infatuation with a girl of fourteen—how Alison Altman, during that rout of my second camp season, came to embody my gothic wantings.

An adult mind, hopeful to interpret and thus reduce, might say I fixed on Alison because she was boy*ish,* boyish, not a boy, not a threat. I could study her, indulge certain inbred fantasies, within what must have looked like the fixed corral of her femaleness.

I plainly see her. Tall, taller than most of the counselors. Flat-chested, lanky and rumpless, washy white skin splatted over with freckles, her black hair cut in little birdwing overlaps that shot blue, as if lightning brewed beneath it . . . she had an up-curved nose, speckly blue, black-lashed eyes. Alison, at fourteen, was still in vague, either-sexed territory, still outside the strictest biology.

She smiled in the frequent way even-tempered people do, so I knew she was unlike me, heavy with mope, peevish, and by my own analysis, newly depraved.

Girls at camp shared the same outdoor sinks and showers. Co-balt-blue Noxema jars and pleated bits of toothpaste tubes littered the shelf above the long metal trough with its dozen or more fat spigots. From my assigned spot in line, to catch sight of Alison spitting out a foamy gob of toothpaste, then tilting her head to swallow water, meant unbearable pleasure.

I set my days like traps for opportunities to see her. During rest time, Denise and I snuck behind a certain building to smoke. It was only by pretending to relish an illicit cigarette that I could again watch Alison, on her stomach in her bunk, reading, elbows grinding into the mattress, fingers hooking through her black hair.

The older girls decided to throw a dance. Somebody'd found blue Christmas lights, looped them through pine branches around the clearing that was to be our dance floor. Somebody else brought out the record player and a stack of 45's. By nine o'clock it was pitchy, cool black out; there must have been thirty girls dancing in a circle lit up like a country bar, ringed around with black swoops of deadpan pines. Alison, in a white shirt and jeans, looked gawkish, beautifully dopey when she danced, minus the emergent sexuality of the other girls her age. She moved with lazy good nature, the way she did everything. My friends and I danced, falling short of sophistication by a mile. But we twisted, jump-hopped, and howled within the bluish clearing because somebody said we could, because we were awed by the older girls and were their natural imitators.

In a spirit of mischief or, who knows, even wishful thinking, someone slipped on a slow, achey song, the kind where boys and girls curl together like mating insects, barely moving. The kind my mother took severe objection to. The darkness helped. Watching other girls dance together. With my need shoving me forward, I went up to Alison, asked her to dance. We entwined hands, her arm strapped loosely around my waist, she took the boy's part. I was a dumb show of extremes, of temperatures and feelings, which caused me to move and act all the more rigidly. I wouldn't speak or look up at her. Our bodies softly bumped, moths against the light of one another.

Maybe somebody got a little embarrassed or confused by that slow, close dancing, because afterward there was only wild, loud music, and everyone went back to frenzied, uncoupled dancing. I lost sight of Alison after that.

I took home a couple of addresses and phone numbers, but I never bothered. My mother discovered the dope addict paperback in my suitcase when she was dumping my clothes into the washer. She confronted me, shaking it by one grimy corner. I feigned innocence, countering her fears about me with luridly detailed information about Denise. What was left of the summer looked as if it might be kept afloat by bike rides, tennis lessons, reading books up in my room.

In the kitchen Mother had the phone shoved up to her ear, held there by her hunched shoulder, unscrewing a jar of mayonnaise. She was fixing my lunch when the knife stopped in midair, suspended. Seeing me, Mother lowered her voice, turned her back while she talked. Eventually she swiveled back, knife gliding over the bread, talking in a normal voice about her next bridge luncheon, the half-off swimsuit sale at Saks.

She put a sandwich and glass of milk in front of me, sat down

with her own. Her mood was not shaken—why would it
be . . . she'd heard a piece of bad news, a shock if you were ac-
quainted with the person, but a thin thrill of relief was allowable
since she hadn't *known* the child, and thank God it wasn't one of
her own . . .

Evelyn told me the awfulest thing just now.

What?

You remember that darling Alison Altman? Wasn't she at camp
again with you this year? You know her father used to be your
pediatrician.

Bread swelled in my mouth.

She died, yesterday afternoon. Evelyn heard she'd been playing
ball with her little brothers and sisters and dropped dead—in the
street. Dr. Altman was out in the road on his hands and knees,
trying to blow breath into her. He got her heart started again,
then she was at the hospital, Evelyn says, for three or four hours.
She'd have been a vegetable if she'd lived. Poor thing.

This is how it goes after you. My mother had no idea what she
was saying to me. I could see what she'd intended—to divide a bit
of tragic news over lunch, peel at it like an orange, run our
tongues into its pale, acid sadness. Glad it wasn't us.

I shut the door to my room and lay on my bed. My griefs, up to
then, had been open, consolable. Public. This was mine, and it
mauled me. I kept gasping, as if I were being struck.

After a while I dried off my face, went out to my mother, who
was prying dandelions from the lawn, to say I was riding my bike
over to a friend's.

I usually enjoyed telling people that our house had a cemetery
right smack behind it. Saturdays, when I mowed the grass in
back, gray blips would flash up between the redwood fencing.
There was the inexhaustible joke about having quiet neighbors.
And lying on my bed, late, the radio on, I would get peculiarly
numb, feeling what a short distance I was from rows of graves.

Inevitable, that I would ride between the opened ironwork gates, park my bike . . . my crying now like breath, rhythmic, involuntary, I no longer paid attention . . . I walked a long time in that place. The older gravestones had photographs embedded like ticks, oval in their granite chests, as if there had been some short-lived fad. . .

After Alison died, I grew off-balance, obese with secrets. At one point I went out to a back section of our yard, pulling off my butterfly ring, punching a hole with Mother's trowel, burying it. I didn't know what I meant by that.

Later, when I wanted the ring back, I went out and dug it up. It hadn't altered, hadn't spoiled. I washed off the dirt, and it looked exactly the same.

I'm visiting Mother in her new apartment. We are passing the afternoon while the baby naps and my four-year-old builds waxen slums out of Mother's old bridge decks, sifting through old photographs and Christmas cards. It is Mother who finds the Altmans' Christmas pictures. Dr. A. with his wife and a new baby nearly every winter. Alison, an infant propped on her mother's buckle of a lap, then sitting on her father's navy-blue knuckle of a knee, then upright between her fertile parents, displaced by two new babies. I examine her face for some predestination, foreknowledge of early death, but there is only that same even-tempered pleasantness across her features.

My ankles and knees lock among old Christmas messages, bits of picture. I hear myself.

Remember Girl Scout camp, Mom? That second time, when I was twelve? I had some sort of weird crush on her, on Alison. Normal at that age, I guess. Less threatening than a boy . . .

Mother is sifting doggedly on, pulling up other cards and pictures to fatten our nostalgia. My confession has no impact. It loses altitude, falls, overturned, among all the other trivia . . .

What is to confess, then?

Another child picked clean, fed to the body of Life. I learned to face down death, without a word from anyone.

In the busy neglect of growing up, secrets turn porous, shrink to bone.

After bone comes dust.

Oh, Alison.

Spirit Seizures

Based on *The Watseka Wonder,*
an authenticated narrative of spirit
manifestation by Dr. E. W. Stevens, 1908

July 1882: The Binning farm
three miles outside Watseka, Illinois

P̲urplish soil receded in motionless, combed waves from
around the frame house. The ripening corn surged, had an
oily river sheen over it . . .

Holding her newest baby, Lurancy walked again to the road's
edge, shielding her eyes, her sunbonnet tied but swinging against
her damp back. Deep clay ruts crisscrossed the road, old wheel
ruts, but no dust was building in the distance, no buggy approached from town. Mr. Asa B. Roff, a wealthy lawyer, and his
wife Anne, former residents of Watseka, had come from Emporia,
Kansas, to visit their eldest daughter. News that they would also
be visiting the Binnings had bred a quarrel with Lurancy's husband. Thomas had gone down to the river to fish and lay traps,
and to evade further argument. That morning Lurancy had at-

tended both to the baby and their daughter Lucia with over-scrupulous attention, had stiffly set down Thomas's plate of breakfast, avoided watching him eat.

Thomas Binning. In overalls and cracked shoes, that black shingle of hair laid flat across his broad plank of forehead, that infrequent laughter forever reminding her of a saw drawn backward. Now he was coldly separate; her hands served, his took. There could be little else with the Roffs about to visit them again.

Two summers before, the Roffs had returned to Watseka from their new home in Emporia. Lurancy Vennum Binning, as a new bride, had been proud to show her new home, that first child lifting up her belly. Thomas had nearly undone that pride, sitting in their barren front parlor, his knees sprung like an iron scissors, his hands flopped like wrung hens. He sat, stonily ignorant, in that darkened room with Mr. and Mrs. Roff and their daughter Minerva, leaving with a hard curse when Minerva Roff tremblingly proposed that the soul of her sister Mary be brought forward through the able instrument of their dear Lurancy.

Lurancy had already confessed to Thomas about the summer she was thirteen, the night in July 1877 when the voices had started. Hissing voices, breaths clawing over her face . . . *Lurancy, Rancy* . . . a dissonant choir of the dead stopped only by her mother's presence. Then followed seizures, trances, ecstasies, her body rigid while her voice roamed among the contents of heaven. Dead but unreconciled souls borrowed her voice, pressed grievance through her, sour from desuetude.

With everyone, family, physicians, ministers, neighbors, banded under the sad resolve to commit Lurancy Vennum to the Springfield asylum, the Roffs, whose own daughter Mary had been subject to similar seizures before she died in 1865, brought a spiritualist down from Janesville. In the presence of Dr. E. W. Stevens, Mr. and Mrs. Vennum, and Asa Roff, the soul of Mary Roff, dead twelve years, asserted its benign, wonderful residence within Lurancy's flesh. From February to May 1878, Mary's spirit read like wildest news out of the living envelope of Lurancy Ven-

num. While living at the Vennum house, Mary asked repeatedly
to be taken home. With the Vennums' consent, Mary was returned "home," to the Roffs. In late May this personality, soul, or
spirit of Mary Roff vacated Lurancy Vennum and willingly returned to "heaven and angels." Lurancy was escorted back to the
Vennum house, recovered in all her senses.

Thomas Binning had understood nothing. Lurancy's voice had
boiled through him, leaving him empty of all but the most sedi-
mentary opinion that spiritualists were deluded fools. He cared
for Lurancy Vennum only as he knew her, present before his eyes.
Ordinary.

✳ ✳ ✳

Churned white butter, a sweaty caul over it, hung down the
well. Two cakes, wrapped in cloth pale as cerements, lay like tiny
mummies across the cookstove. Lurancy went out to cut oxeye
sunflower, unrolling gaudy bunches of it from her apron, placing
them in a stone crock on the kitchen windowsill and a pewter
pitcher in the front parlor. The house otherwise stood plain, un-
softened by material prosperity.

(Lurancy's family had moved from Milford to Watseka the summer she turned seven, the same summer Martin Meara was
hanged for tying his son across a hot stove because he had not, it
was said by way of explanation, ploughed his day's portion.
Townspeople, mostly men and boys, had ridden out to see the
hanging, brought back pieces of the hackberry tree. Hackberry
branches, to be whittled by morbid hands, or thrillingly revolved
down in dusty, worn pockets.)

Out on the porch steps Lurancy shook out her wavy black hair
(*troughed as a washboard,* her mother would say), refastened it
with the several tortoise combs her mother had given her on her
wedding day. Lucia ran about on the planked porch, cradling the
wood doll Thomas had fashioned for her. A wasp tagged near and
Lurancy slapped at it with the hem of her gingham dress as she
went past, joggling the baby, pacing restlessly from porch side to

porch side, from road's edge to house and back, waiting for her friends . . .

* * *

Pinned beneath a glary noon light, Lurancy held the baby in one arm, yanked the wooden wagon along with the other, Lucia bobbing in it, her sunbonnet hiding her diamond fleck of face, the picnic hamper rocking beside her. In the hamper Lurancy had put cold chicken, bread and butter slices, raspberries, and, in a conciliatory mood, one of the company cakes. The rift with Thomas had broken her peace, and she had no temperament to sustain any quarrel.

Scores of crows were raiding the white, blowing wheat. In turn, they would eat the grasshoppers. To everything a season and time. A solitary crow hopped boldly near them; Lucia cried out, afraid of the obsidian bird and its rapacious sideways eye.

The meadow was full-lit, porous and greenly translucent as a luna moth's wing. Clover was rampant, its puffy thick heads slewed like hail. The Iroquois River glittered behind a long shoulder of trees, a black collar tatted out of the trunks and shade running along its bottom. Dragonflies clicked, netted iridescence passing through a hot canvas of air. Lurancy stopped to pick some tickseed, the tattered gold ruffs and red eye. When Lucia complained, Lurancy set down the flowers, the baby, and lifted her from the wagon, helping her ruck up her skirts and squat. Sweet-smelling urine pooled into the seeding grasses.

Lurancy pulled the wagon toward a familiar break in the trees, the elms and maples, to the narrow path down which Thomas would have gone to fish.

His back was to them, standing by the dun, high-banked river, water both she and her brothers had been baptized in.

Thomas.

From his face, turned first on Lucia, then to herself, Lurancy perceived, and gratefully, that he had no stock in further argument.

They sat peaceably, ate what she had brought. She opened her dress to feed the baby. Thomas had caught a string of fish, shot two mallards, drakes.

The Roffs have not come.

Maybe they lost their way? He was teasing, yet so honestly hopeful that she laughed.

You should use the mallard or the fish if they'll be staying over for supper, Rancy.

Yes.

She knotted back her skirts, rinsed the pewter dishes in the river. Thomas stood nearby, holding the baby; when she lost a dish to the current, he retrieved it for her.

Thomas had begun, lately, to talk of homesteading. Selling the farm. Of Kansas. Moving to some treeless spot, worlds from anybody, living most likely in a sod hut. Where her life would ebb with the bearing of child upon child. With helping Thomas to tame a bit of tough prairie. Well, she had chosen him. Now he picked the course and rigor of their lives. The Roffs would come, stir up her old self, jog her longing for those wide, fertile talks about spirit worlds, angels, and spirit guides, all things which Thomas opposed, even cursed. (*What you cannot see, do you think you are to know, imagine that you know?*)

Lucia clasped the lank bouquet as the wagon rose and dipped through the meadow. The baby, shaded by the hamper, slept. Over where the farm lay, the sky was a massive block of gray-purple. By the river it would still be sunny and hot. Wind tossed like a wall of water over them. Lurancy's muslin apron buffeted fitfully. Lucia began to cry, covering her ears at the first crack of thunder. A blue skeletal jig of lightning flared. Lurancy dragged at the wagon as fast as she dared without throwing the baby. She could see the wash, make out her own dress and one of Lucia's a-skip on the line as if they were partnered at a town dance. Rain like a scatter of buckshot hit at her face. Pull up your bonnet, Lucia, she yelled over the wind, then pulled up her own.

The air was thick with a greenish, moldery light. Another heaving split of thunder, sounding like a house collapsed, with a crackle of husk beneath it. Trees blew, heeled in one direction, suddenly weak-seeming.

Lurancy strained to make out the shape of an unfamiliar object outside their house. The buggy, the Roffs' buggy, empty, stood outside their porch, the horses' heads dejected, rain stippling their reddish hides. It seemed the whole awash world of the dead had come with these people who would have cause to greet her, perhaps even to love her, then set about drawing their dead child's spirit like spittled thread through the blunt eye of able Lurancy Binning.

Lurancy willed her spirit to loft, untenant, so Mary Roff might enter, impetuously, this world.

> *for all flesh is like*
> *grass*
> *and all its glory like the flower of*
> *grass*
> *but the grass withers, the flower falls*
> *but the word of the Lord will endure*
> *for ever*

Lurancy picked up the baby, grabbed Lucia by the hand, and even with skirts nearly anchored by cold rain and hemmed by river clay, the near-empty vessel of Lurancy Binning pitched lightly up the wide solid steps her husband had built for her, to seek some short respite with those he refused to understand.

1889: Dr. Richard Hodgson,
of the Society for Psychical Research,
listens to Minerva Alter,
forty-six years old and sister
to Mary Roff

. . . Of us five Roff children, Mary stood forth, from the very beginning, as peculiar. Subject to fits, black pressing moods. Which grew increasingly worse, don't you see, to the point where

Mother and Father tried a great many things to cure her. As a girl I can recall the house being overtaken by doctors, ministers, faith healers of all kinds. One remedy working, then another, then nothing.

Mary, when she was well, had a great attachment to music. Solemn dreary tunes out of our Methodist hymnal pleased her most. We tried to tease her out of her preference for such dirges. "What sad, sobering music for a pretty child, Mary," our mother would say, but Mary would turn with her dark eyes from the piano, fix us with those impenetrable eyes. "But it is the exact pace and lyric which pleases me, Mother."

Would you like me to play one of Mary's hymns for you, Doctor? This is the exact piano she used to sit down to. Father gave it to Dr. Alter and myself when they moved out to Emporia. At the time Mary's spirit took up lodging in Miss Vennum, it was nearly the first object she recognized with affection when she stepped back into our family home. But it had been twelve years since her death, don't you see, so her fingers would not work over the keys with any of the grace they had once possessed, and for that she sweetly and, faintly troubled, apologized . . .

Here, if I remember, is a favorite of Mary's before she died, aged eighteen years:

> *How blest is our brother bereft*
> *Of all that could burthen his mind!*
> *How easy the soul, that hath left*
> *The wearisome body behind!*
> *This languishing head is at rest,*
> *Its thinking and aching are o'er,*
> *This quiet immovable breast*
> *Is heaved by affliction no more . . .*

For over a year Mary was sent off to Peoria, to the water cures. Again, it seemed to help, until the melancholia and fits returned. Most of our backwoods physicians still treated any overstimulation of the body by leeching. Mary herself took to placing leeches against her temples, to take away the "lump of pain," as she called it. There the leeches would lie, growing from cool to warm, flat to swollen, till they dropped off, all sated. And Mary would collect them into jars, treat them almost as her playthings *(rusty-black, wormy, eyeless creatures, like something the Devil might scheme to create)*. Dr. Alter never held to the idea of cupping or leeching, thought it old-fashioned and dangerous to debilitate a weak person with fasting or draining of vital blood.

. . . Why yes, Dr. Hodgson, I do remember that one particular afternoon you refer to. Awful. Awful, discovering my sister in the back yard, just under some bushes. All bloody, nearly dead. She'd taken a kitchen knife and gone into the yard, deliberately cut into her arm. You must have heard then, Doctor, that part of the story where Mary's spirit, while in the bodily vehicle of Miss Vennum, went to show Dr. Stevens the knife-scar along her arm, then remembered, saying, oh, this is not the one, that other arm is in the ground, then described to him her burial, named the mourners standing about her grave . . .

Oh, stories did circulate and abound, details of Mary's spirit-return, her uncanny recall of old neighbors, past occasions, things no one but Mary Roff herself could have recalled.

Before passing back into the Borderland that May of 1878, Mary wanted Lurancy to be given certain small tokens, a few cards, some marbles, 25¢, Mary, you see, being grateful to Lurancy. This I did.

The first time I met my sister after her death? That would be February 1878: Mother and I were walking down Sixth Street to pay a visit to the Vennums, having heard about their oldest girl's strange seizures so much like Mary's had been, her repeated claim to be Mary Roff. Before Mother, I noticed the girl leaning out from the top story of their small, rather shabby house, waving and calling "Nervie, Nervie!" Always Mary's nickname for me. The voice was exactly Mary's.

At our parents' house over those next three months, Mary and I spent many hours recalling childhood; or rather, Mary remembered while I affirmed. Pranks, for instance the time she and one of our younger cousins tried to rub a made-up ointment into the sore eyes of one of our hens. She remembered that.

Mary's spirit, at the beginning, refused food. At table she bowed her head, murmuring that she supped in heaven; but as the body of Miss Vennum regained its vigor, so did Mary begin to eat. That spring I accompanied Mother and Mary into many of our finest homes in Watseka. I was accustomed soon enough to being overlooked while all flocked to see the proof of Mary in young Lurancy Vennum . . . and rarely were disappointed.

In the years before her death, Mary was famous in Watseka and beyond for her fits and clairvoyances. Blindfolded, she read newspapers aloud, read sealed letters, then arranged boxes of letters alphabetically, things of that sort. Newspapermen, well-to-do townspeople, even Mayor Secrest and his wife, all paid ceaseless visits to our home, until our very lives revolved around Mary's peculiar orb, and by her reflection we were cast into that same unnatural light.

After she died, July the 5th, 1865, our lives took up some normalcy. I met Dr. Alter, we were married, I continued teaching Sunday school. He practiced the medicine he'd learned on the East Coast and in Boston. He was popular here in Watseka, with his new ideas and theories . . . yet these couldn't save our own children. When black diphtheria came through Milford, then Watseka, we watched our innocent children, six of our seven, sicken and succumb. Three taken in the span of one night. Dr. Alter made a slit in Ada's windpipe, trying to bring air to her lungs; without result he did the same for little Charles. Which of us was the more bereft by the loss in one week, of six of our children, myself still nursing Asa, who died in my arms, or my husband, being unable to save one of them? It was quick, beyond control; he was as helpless as I was.

If you would be so kind as to follow me, Dr. Hodgson, to the table over by the window, you can see what gives me peace at times . . . this is hair from each one of our children. Ada's. Frederick's. Here is Maude's. Mary's. Charlie. Even little Asa, who had such a crop of it and so black. As they died in turn, Mother went into their rooms for me, cutting their hair. I plait and twist, like this, shaping the hair into patterns, bouquets . . . when I finished that first time, pain welled up and so maddeningly that I was compelled to tear the bouquet apart, almost frantically, and begin again.

More often than Dr. Alter, I visit the gravebeds at Oak Hill *(those pickets, a pale set of tongues swelling up from the earth).*

Yes. Well yes, he did. A seventh child, Robert, did survive. With his wife and five children he lives just outside Milford, a carpenter. Robert was left to raise, but I hadn't much heart for it . . . looking at him, I saw the others. Wondered why him spared, and not even my favorite. Many families lost children that winter; I suppose we were not singled out except in the extremity of our loss.

I have heard, as others have written it to me, that Lurancy Binning lives out in Kansas, Rawlins County, mother to six or seven. Those episodes in her early life nearly forgotten, occupied as she is with the obligations of rearing children, raising up living children . . .

As a physician, of course, my husband has slipped back into the lively stream of need and fulfillment of need. But since Mary, since my own children were taken, I savor so little. The spiritual cannot console me, perhaps from being over-long exposed to it. I am most content up at Oak Hill. Or in turning their hair to glinting shapes, vines.

I am removed from nature's lures, numb to its cruel trees, cruel birds, cruel river water, to its food, or to any fine thing. A bead-strand of monotony before my eyes. I have, as you see for yourself, been carted off by grief.

I would gain no benefit by lying to you or to anyone about my sister Mary. I care little what others beyond this place say of the case of Mary Roff or the "Watseka Wonder," as Miss Vennum is at times called. Mary's soul returned to us that one time, then briefly, twice more, when Mother and Father and I visited the Binning farm. Lurancy's husband, unaccustomed to our spiritualist beliefs, was neither welcoming nor hospitable; yet she seemed exceedingly joyful to see us. I remember that. How she pressed her children upon me, quite thoughtlessly *(agonizing, the sight of tiny, still-animate faces).*

I will walk with you over to our family home. You will want to talk with my brother and his family. No, I prefer not. I will go on to Oak Hill.

(Where all one day will assemble in plain, purblind rows, under sober ineloquent stone, our lives reduced to that faint quaver of rumour . . . where some hundred years from now, we may persist, a source of curiosity and likely, some little disbelief . . .)

Well now.

It has been nearly a lifting of some burden, to speak to you of these things.

MARY ROFF

I'm gonna take a trip on that old gospel ship
I'm goin' far beyond the sky
I'm gonna shout and sing, til the bell done ring
When I bid this world good-bye

What is a House but a hundred boards upended and smacked together, the ten hammers which plowed the humid air, the cracking of hammers, the thundering which resides in the air around the loosening nails, the dark fingerspaces between . . . ? And what is a town but fifty such buildings, lined up and stopping short . . . ending with my House, which goes only so far across the thickened ground to overlook the flat river . . . ? What is a town such as this but a hastily reassembled forest, trees felled, taken into measured pieces and put back together in such a way that they might move about in them secretly, sleep, fight, take supper, increase their poor numbers, instead of standing outside, looking up a solid, impenetrable trunk, awed and displaced?

And what is Bodily Flesh but a house so lightly mortised as to permit an occasional strike of soul to flash through like summer lightning? Mary Roff. I was that white, half-empty pitcher, born unwhole, unfinished, as a baby comes without its hearing or its proper sight, missing some symmetry of limb, so I did enter the clayey sphere of weights and dimensions, unfinished. No one saw that I was a soul not fixedly mortised. That older, swifter souls slid in and out of me, bats in an abandoned and shifting outbuilding. I was an incompleteness pouring like oil or watered wine between two vessels, a shiny arc rocking between one named assembly of flesh and another, and near the end, poured from Mary into Lurancy, and back from Lurancy poured yet again into Mary . . . a child's game, going in and out the windows . . .

If you are ashamed of me, you ought not to be
And you'd better have a care,
If too much fault you find, you'll sure be left behind
When I'm sailing through the air

And what was Lurancy Vennum Binning but that vulnerable, slight growth latched onto by heavy, malevolent souls, then turned by me into a woman yoked to toil, to the magnetism of scraping her nourishment from dirt? I was glad for her to have husband-love and child-love, what I never knew, being encumbered by an oppression of spirits all crowding into the closet of one body as if it were some great vibrating hall.

And what, then, of Nervie, my sister Nervie, but a high-spirited woman, unable to tolerate either flesh or spirit, a woman pos-

sessed of no convictions but those passive ones of grief and loss—
she grew attached to loss, dependent on sorrow, came to love
them dearer than anything.

What is Soul or Spirit but Mystery, a Glory Ship, that Rumour
founded by tales such as mine—Mad Mary Roff—tales bringing
not confirmation but bare continuance of hope . . . instructing
humanity in its keenest question: But if a man die, shall he live
again?

> *I have good news to bring*
> *And that is why I sing,*
> *All my joys with you I'll share*
> *I'm gonna take a trip on that old Gospel Ship*
> *And go sailing through the air*

Previous Winners of
THE FLANNERY O'CONNOR AWARD
FOR SHORT FICTION

David Walton, *Evening Out*
Leigh Allison Wilson, *From the Bottom Up*
Sandra Thompson, *Close-Ups*
Susan Neville, *The Invention of Flight*
Mary Hood, *How Far She Went*
François Camoin, *Why Men Are Afraid of Women*
Molly Giles, *Rough Translations*
Daniel Curley, *Living with Snakes*
Peter Meinke, *The Piano Tuner*
Tony Ardizzone, *The Evening News*
Salvatore La Puma, *The Boys of Bensonhurst*